THE ULTIMATE GOOD LUCK

"Richard Ford's Harry Quinn has come to the Mexican city of Oaxaca to buy his ex-lover Rae's brother Sonny out of jail. Sonny has been found in a hotel room with a lot of cocaine. The dealer he was running for believes Sonny was double-crossing him. The moves in the game take place in an archaic world of drug dealers and crook lawyers. It is not the only world in the city of Oaxaca, however. The native poor and urban guerrillas are victims of one another, and of the police and army. American tourists, like visitors to a game reserve, are the occasional casualties of passing violence . . . The book brings to mind cinematic versions of the romance of urban dereliction – the look of *Paris, Texas* for example . . . You want Wim Wenders to make the movie, but you want Bogart and Bacall to be in it"

PETER CAMPBELL, *London Review of Books*

"Ford's taut, compelling prose is as piercingly clear as a police siren. No other storyteller writes about the alienated and uncommitted with such mastery"   PENNY PERRICK, *Sunday Times*

"So hardboiled and tough that it might have been written on the back of a trenchcoat. A grand *Maltese Falcon* of a novel"

STANLEY ELKIN

"Ford's sense of place is extraordinary. This is the work of a formidably talented novelist"   *Newsweek*

RICHARD FORD was born in Jackson, Mississippi, in 1944. His first novel, *A Piece of My Heart*, was runner up for the Ernest Hemingway Award in 1976. *The Ultimate Good Luck* was followed by *The Sportswriter* and *Wildlife*, which Salman Rushdie described as "a fine novel by a fine writer". It was *The Sportswriter* which affected a whole decade for writers and readers, and to which *Independence Day*, which was awarded the 1995 Pulitzer Prize for fiction and the PEN/Faulkner Award, is the sequel. Richard Ford's collection of stories *Rock Springs* was described in the *Sunday Times* as "a collection of stunning impact . . ."

Kristina
and for
Edna Ford

Richard Ford

THE ULTIMATE GOOD LUCK

THE HARVILL PRESS
LONDON

I am grateful to the John Simon Guggenheim Foundation
and to the National Endowment for the Arts, who supported
me generously while I wrote this book.   R. F.

A portion of this book appeared in *TriQuarterly*

First published in Great Britain by Collins Harvill in 1989

This paperback edition first published in 1996
by The Harvill Press, 2 Aztec Row, Berners Road, London N1 0PW

www.harvill.com

3 5 7 9 8 6 4 2

© 1981 by Richard Ford

Richard Ford asserts the moral right to be identified as the author of this work

A CIP catalogue record for this book is available from the British Library

ISBN 1 86046 174 3

Typeset in Bembo

Printed and bound in Great Britain by Mackays of Chatham

Half title illustration by CDT Design Ltd

1

QUINN KNEW HE NEEDED to get lucky.

Rae was coming from Mexico City in the afternoon, and if they placed the money right, Sonny stepped out of the prisión three days later and disappeared.

Luck, Quinn thought, was always infatuated with efficiency. A Persian proverb said that very thing. And since he'd been in Oaxaca, he'd been efficient to every stinking particular. He'd been efficient, in fact, if he hadn't been anything else. The only thing he couldn't be sure about—and it worried him—was if it still ran in his character to get lucky.

In the afternoon he had met an Italian girl in the Portal de Flores. She had wandered out of the park through the street tables as though she was looking for someone in particular, and sat at his table. She smiled when she sat down and turned and looked back up the Portal at the hippies and the blanket beggars and the English tourists having coffees. She looked at him and smiled confidingly, as if he should understand why she was there. Quinn had begun to make it a habit to have no nonessential conversations. Talk was risky. You couldn't tell what you'd say, and seven months alone had taught him to be quiet. But he didn't mind sitting across from her. Nobody got pregnant looking. The Portal boundaried the central park with a long vaulted commercial arcade with the interior side open. It was the center of evil and good commerce in Oaxaca. He met Bernhardt in the Portal on the days they went to the prison, waiting underneath the suspended Raleigh package for Bernhardt's Mercedes to turn the corner into Hidalgo Street. And on days they didn't go to the prison, he liked to come down in the early evening when the Centro wasn't full of fresh tourists and the light was chartreuse and less precise and there seemed to be a kind of small impersonal welcoming life in the streets, a sense of confidence that everything you saw was functioning predictably.

The girl was in her early twenties with a round Scandinavian face that didn't make her pretty, but made her plainness appealing. Her mouth had dark expressive lips. She took a pair of sandals out of her bolsa and worked on the straps awhile without speaking, and finally put them on. Quinn read *Excelsior* for the ball scores. The girl looked back down the Portal and tried to get the attention of a waiter but couldn't. She looked at Quinn again and smiled and asked for a cigarette. When she had begun smoking she asked where he was from and he only told her the States. She said, blowing smoke, she was from Milano and had been in Oaxaca a week resting up. She said she had come down from Mexico City with a friend in a van and he had left her and gone, and that she was waiting one more day for him, then taking a bus to San Cristóbal, where she knew people. She had thick brown hair with a green ribbon braided into one thin strand. She thought it was her nicest feature. She kept running the backs of her fingers through it as though it was getting in her way, which it didn't. She seemed prettier when she talked, and he didn't mind listening to her. She asked him why he was in Oaxaca, and he said he was a tourist. She told him the best Zapotec ceramics were in the poor pueblos beyond Mitla, and the best dyed woolens were sold in the mountains near Teotitlán, and that the best mescal was made in the fábricas away from town, and that only shit was for sale in the Juárez Market. She asked him how many plaquettes of quaaludes he thought it would be safe to send back to the States

2

in the mail without arousing suspicion, and he told her he couldn't guess, and she seemed satisfied that the idea didn't upset him.

Quinn began watching her. She wasn't Italian, but that didn't matter. She could be Pennsylvania Dutch for the difference it would make, and moving quaaludes into the States didn't make you dangerous. He doubted she was even doing it, or she wouldn't have asked. It was just a way to make life interesting when you're bored and broke, which he thought she was. She hadn't made a serious attempt to get a waiter, and was waiting for an offer. He liked the way her face darted up and down when she talked, so that her features turned appealing then plain then appealing again depending on whether she smiled. The change back to appealing surprised him every time, and he kept looking for it. She was the first woman he had talked to in a month, and he wondered which face you'd see late at night and which one you'd remember. Since Rae had left he had a habit of only remembering the bad ones. He asked her if she wanted a mescal and she said she did and smiled.

After an hour the Portal began to empty. The Americans left for cocktails at the Victoria, and the hippies faded away to the sleazy hotels back of the market. It was the time of day he liked best in Mexico, a time he never liked in Michigan. In Michigan things were finished now, but in Mexico action was just beginning again. He wanted to stay until the army band started up in the park, and then he was going to the fights.

The girl stopped talking, as if she hoped something interesting would happen. She asked for another cigarette and sat back in her chair with one arm on the table and watched the park empty of tourists. She had no place to go, that much was clear. She was slumming. But he didn't know if he should take a chance. Women had been off the routine since he'd arrived. They pushed things out of shape too fast. Everything you relied on could tip. Whole empires had gone over for smaller risks. But sometimes you had to adjust your routine to serve the circumstances, and the circumstances added up that he wanted the girl to stay.

3

When he had sat for a while without speaking, he asked her if she'd like to go across to the Monte Albán and eat the comida and go to the fights. He had been watching the posters on the comerciales all week, and he wanted to see a fight. He liked Mex fights. He had a memory of the chicos in Michigan, down between the long barracks houses in the cherry groves, north of Traverse City. He would sneak out late at night and stand in the tight circles and watch the slender shirtless boys go bare knuckles in the kerosene light. They were stand-up and correct fights, and the punches drew blood precisely. The boys whispered while they fought in the hot dirt, until one boy couldn't get up, then everyone in the circle would close and pick him up formally, and file back into the whitewashed houses to get drunk, and he'd be left alone in the dark with his heart pounding. It was always a war, and he didn't remember cowards. Cowardice seemed as far away as death, and when it was over you felt lucky, even left by yourself.

The girl laughed strangely when he mentioned the fights and glanced around her at the empty tables down the Portal where the waiters were standing motionless. Some street boys had begun to hustle a fat German woman for change. The woman batted her hand at them as if they were flies. Things, Quinn felt, would be starting up again in an hour.

The idea of a fight seemed to confuse her. It wasn't what she had expected to be offered. Light had died in the Centro in the time she had sat there. The air was cool and plum tinted in shadows along the Portal. Traffic had cleared. The Zapotec women in the plaza had taken their backstrap looms down off the benches and were packing them in bundles. The afternoon was over, and the day, he thought, probably looked different to her now from when she sat down. It was a bad time to have to be alone someplace. He could tell she felt that. The military band had begun to muster below the raised kiosk. The musicians stood patiently, holding their instruments, waiting for someone to unlock the low door. They seemed remote and practical.

The girl was broke, and what he had in mind for her didn't

4

matter to her much. She only wanted to take a last reading on the day before giving it up and starting the night with a stranger. You made the best arrangements you could, and that always meant having a last look around. He wasn't in a hurry. Through the whitewashed trees he watched a photographer haul his wooden pony across the park. He thought it would be nice to have a picture made.

When she had stared across the Portal for a while she bit her lip and looked at him as if he was the owner of a dangerous car that would take her a long way from where she wanted to go, but would get her there fast.

"Why do you want to go to the fights?" she asked and smiled curiously.

"I guess I've gotten desperate since the ballet left," he said, and smiled back.

"I'll bet you have," she said.

"Do you want to go?" He folded his paper and laid it on the table.

"Do you want me to stay with you tonight?" she asked. She bit her lip again and looked at him brightly. It was her idea now, and everything came up front. She liked it tidy, no mysteries, and she had his number, like a smart fourteen-year-old.

"I've got business in the morning," he said, "but I'll work it out."

Her face took on the appealing look. It made him feel smart. "Everyone has business," she said. She began putting her shoes back in her bolsa. "Why would you stay here otherwise? It's so boring. Nothing ever happens. I'm sorry I ever came. But I'm here now." She smiled again.

"I'll try to keep you busy," he said.

"That'll be great," she said as she stood up.

✳

The arena de boxeo was a small unventilated warehouse on the American Highway past the last streetlights at the edge of the barrio popular. The Italian girl drank mescalitos at dinner, and complained a lot about the Mexican men whom she didn't care for and how her father had a lot of money in Milano except she couldn't stand him, and had come to live with her mother in New York and had taken up with the wrong people in Mexico. It seemed to make her sad. The hot air inside the arena had the high pomade and liniment smell of little boxing-club halls in East L.A., from the time he'd first known Rae two years ago, air with risk in it, palpable and utterly in the present, and going right into it made him feel lucky, which was how he wanted to feel.

In the ring two Zapotec boys were feeling each other out, circling uncomfortably beneath a bluish light that seemed to make the middle of the warehouse fall below a dense black cloud. Neither boy was a boxer, and neither one wanted to get hurt. Their long, stiff jabs made their gloves dip and seem heavy, like big red balloons, and they moved without discipline and too slowly to want to fight. They were friends, Quinn thought, and that made everything too hard. It was hard to want to kill your friend. The Mexicans in the arena didn't approve. They were drinking mescal and yelling, though the boys were oblivious. He wanted this fight to be over and better fighters to come in, and so did the Mexicans. The Italian girl had quit talking and stared up at the ring as if someone she knew was inside and something maybe funny would happen to him. She was drunk and having dreams already, and he wanted her to keep together.

The noise in the arena began to grow loud, and both boys' handlers thumped their elbows on the apron and started yelling at them in Zapotec. The blue light made both fighters seem slow and inconclusive, and everyone realized all at once that the fight wasn't going to work out.

A large man stood up suddenly in the back rows and threw a pop bottle that hit the ropes and bounced on the canvas, hitting the taller of the two boys in the foot. The boy stopped circling and put down his hands to look at where the bottle had stopped spinning beside his foot. He seemed concerned, and turned to the

6

referee as if he wanted to have the bottle removed before going on. The referee glared into the crowd, wanting to find who had thrown the bottle. He was a short man in a white sweat-stained shirt and a toothbrush mustache, and he seemed to be annoyed. The taller boy began pointing with his glove, and the handler of the second fighter began screaming and beating the apron with his fists, and the boy suddenly threw a straight-in, leaning right with his thumb extended, and hit the taller boxer in the temple just below his hairline, knocking him backward off his feet into the ropes. He came down hard on the seat of his trunks, heels off the floor, and Quinn could see that the boy's eye had been sprung out of its socket by the other boy's thumb, and that it was hung out of his face by filaments.

"Oh please," the Italian girl gasped. "Just please now, I don't like this, just please." She put her hands up to her face and rocked backward so that he got afraid she would fall off the bench. It was just a pug's trick, he had seen it worked before. It looked plenty bad, but it wasn't as bad as it looked. A good corner could put the eye back, and two stitches would hold it in. Except the Italian girl didn't know that, and it began to seem like a good idea to get her out before she got crazy.

The boy with his eye out pulled himself up on the ropes and began walking stiffly around the ring, his hands on his hips, as if he were walking off a charley horse, only with his head down so that the eye swung a little on whatever was holding it. Quinn couldn't see anything behind him except a thick swarming black-ness. The Mexicans were all stunned and silent while they tried to figure if an important enough decorum had been offended and what they ought to do about it. The referee was trying to get the injured boy to stop walking and was hugging his short arms around the boy's chest, but the boy kept going. The other boxer stood in the neutral corner with his arms draped on the ropes, talking down to his handlers, who were making fists and yelling some-thing very emphatically. The Italian girl had begun to cry quietly, and he wished she could disappear.

7

The boy with his eye out all at once stopped walking and swooned back into the ropes as though he had fainted. None of his handlers would get into the ring. The referee produced a pink handkerchief and was trying to cradle the boy's eye back up toward the socket but didn't quite seem to understand the mechanics. The boy still had his mouthpiece, and he was bleeding from his nose and blood was sprinkling on his knees and starting to track in the sweat. He moved his legs to stand up, but they didn't seem to have any strength left.

The Italian girl wouldn't speak and had become rigid in her seat. Quinn wanted to move out of the arena.

The boy in the neutral corner began to survey the crowd casually. His handlers were talking fast and counting off something on their fingers that the boy was apparently supposed to hear but didn't. He looked bemused, and he worked his mouthpiece and his knees automatically as if he expected the fight to start again but didn't care when. His eyes were fixed, and his face looked calm. He seemed to be thinking about something far away. Suddenly he waved his glove at the men who were counting, turned toward the ring, and ran and hit the injured boy again flush in the face, knocking him off his knees onto his side, and began dancing around the center of the canvas holding his arms up. The referee started waving his arms, and the Italian girl out of instinct was moving away from where she was, straight into the men beside her, saying "con permiso, con permiso," and then a folding chair hit the air and the crowd began screaming, and police appeared, pushing toward the ring, and Quinn knew he had to get out. He couldn't risk police, and he began shoving the girl through the crowd toward where he thought a door was, trying to get himself back into the night before something worse happened and before he had pissed away everything.

✳

In the bungalow the girl wanted to do everything, as though going to the fights had been her bad idea for a good time and not his,

8

and she wanted to put it right. She took off her clothes in the living room without talking, took a lude, then got on her knees beside the davenport and licked him down his legs and up his chest and his arms and blew him in an expert way that made him come fast. She drank some mescal out of a bottle in her bolsa and took a crossroads, then walked him into the bedroom as though the house was hers and turned on the lights and sat on the side of the bed and looked like she wanted to apologize for something. She was a smaller girl with her clothes off, with turned-up breasts and thin legs. Her hair seemed thicker in the light, and when he got in bed with her she climbed on him and fucked him until she worked herself down into her pill and the mescal, down below whatever she'd seen in the boxing ring that was making her want to apologize. It hadn't been what she bargained for, but he thought she was the kind of girl who made the most of things, and he admired her for it, though he had lost any philosophy that made it possible to feel sorry for her. When she was finished, she got off him and went to the bathroom, and came back with a wet cloth and wiped it over his legs, and in a little while she lay back on the pillow in the light and went to sleep.

At two o'clock he got out of bed, turned off the light and did pushups till his arms ached, then walked out onto the walled patio where he could see the city against the black Sierra and breathe the bougainvillea. In the war, this was scrounge time, when things got dicey. The incomings wasted you out of sleep, slammed your face in the dirt, clawing the deck for a flak vest and helmet. He didn't want to be asleep at two o'clock anymore. He preferred to be alert to whatever there was to hear. The bungalow sat on a long, eucalyptus-shaded hill that humped back toward the big mountains north of town. It was the suburbs. Americans rented there because the bungalows were cheap and neat and had grassy lawns and no deposits were taken. But he didn't know the American girls next door, and now that Rae was coming with the money, and the hard part was done and Sonny was coming out, he wouldn't have the chance. He had begun, in a month of waiting and passing

9

through offices and anterooms, and seven months living alone, to feel like he was losing a freedom of some kind, getting cautious without any gain back in precision. Bernhardt said it was the American experience abroad, the long decline in expectation until you could see the immediate world like a native, but without the native's freedom. It should be a great unburdening, Bernhardt said, but to Americans it was always a hardship. Bernhardt thought Americans thrived on protecting privileges nobody else would ever want. Bernhardt liked explanations. It was a lawyer's vice.

Oaxaca sparkled like a matrix of platinum sequins laid over velvet. The dark played out into the valley south toward Chiapas, so that where the land stopped and the sky began was a boundary lost to sight. He counted landmarks every night. The pink rotator on the airport tower, the blue Corona Cerveza on Bustamante, the hollow lights that shone all night on the cathedral opposite the zócalo, and the red Pepsi script shimmering far out in the Mixtec barrios beyond the river. There was never a sense of intimacy. The town seemed to function practically in the visible distance, though the empty air in between became enticing and silent and still. The American Highway curled down the mountains, split, circled the city two ways, then reunited, and the only detectable movement there was the lights of an overland truck gearing down before flatting out into the valley. Americans were off the road hours ago. The trucks and the Dinas would blink their lights, then run you off the cliffsides.

Quinn thought when you hung out in the present, which he did, you slipped free of the past, though not the future, and all the anxieties came in at higher calibers. It was why he liked fucking phony Italian girls from the Portal, and why he'd let Rae leave when she got ready. Too much future, too much anxiousness. In the present, he knew precisely how it would all feel every time: the contact, then the being alone, then somebody else coming in to fill up the space. That was manageable, and you felt lucky and not anxious, and when it wasn't done right, like this time, it didn't matter. Except for Rae. Rae had left a space he couldn't quite manage anymore. And he'd come down for Sonny just to get Rae, since Rae seemed essential to the present, and since he was tired of being alone with himself. Efficiency only took you so far.

Her letter had said, "Dear Harry, No phone? Are you still up there protecting the animals in silence? If so, could you bear to protect one more? (That was my joke, though jokes aren't your long suit.) I apologize for saying Sonny's in trouble in Mexico. Needs money. Needs help. It's me who needs protecting. Could you do this one? Could you, would you? I think there's still a chance. Call me on Long Island. Love Rae. (remember me?)"

He had closed up the trailer in two days.

Inside the bungalow the Italian girl was having a bad time. The mescal willies. She turned and threw her arms up in a mescal dream. It made you feel like you were falling through water where there wasn't any bottom to reach. She called out, "Please don't get in bed with me, will you please not, please." He wondered if she was dreaming about him or about the boy with his eye thumbed out or about somebody even worse.

He watched another truck wind down the American Highway, let his eyes widen in the darkness. He'd be happy once Rae came back and they could get out. That was all he cared about now. The fights hadn't made him feel lucky, but they hadn't bummed anything either, and that was acceptable. It could be worse. He heard dogs barking down in the Reforma. A bitch was in heat, and all the other dogs were enjoying it.

He walked back inside. The Italian girl was sitting in bed in the dark, smoking a cigarette.

"I don't know why I came up here with you," she said. She was angry, and she was getting ready to split. He sat on the wooden chair and wondered how she'd get back down the hill to town. "You meet a lot of people traveling," she said coldly. "People you wouldn't think of passing time with somewhere else." She blew more smoke into the air and watched him in the dark. She seemed sorry about a lot of things all at once. "I sucked you off, right?" she said. "And I don't even know your name."

"Harry Quinn," he said. He tried to think of a funny name, but couldn't come up with one funny enough. It didn't make any difference. She was just a bimbo, and she knew it, and she was pissed about it. He couldn't blame her. She hadn't had first-rate treatment.

"You could be a policeman, you know," she said. "I'm smuggling fucking ludes and crossroads and you could bust me, and where would I be?"

"Looking at you, you'd probably still be right here," Quinn said. He wanted to give her her due, but he didn't want to be up all night sympathizing. He knew he should've gotten her out before she went to sleep.

"That's the problem for foreigners in a strange country," she said.

"What's that?" he said.

"A frame of reference," she said. "You lack a frame of reference that allows you to take the right mental picture. I'd never know if you were a fucking federale until it was too late. You could be a federale for all I know, and I'd be in the prisión with all the other assholes." She mashed the cigarette out on the wall behind her. He thought he could end it better than this. He wanted to go back to sleep, but thought he might've waited too long. "I trusted you," she said, and cleared her throat of smoke. "You know trust is at the heart of love and art and all kinds of shit. And you could have just had me off. What does that shitty tattoo say on your arm?"

"Good conduct," Quinn said. "It's supposed to keep me out of trouble. But it doesn't work."

"Well I think you're an asshole," she said. "Only asshole trash have tattoos. You and your fucking muscles."

"Why don't you go back down the hill?" he said. "I'll get up and drive you." He thought he could win back an hour or two if she was gone.

"Just forget it," she said, and slid back down under the covers.

He didn't understand why the girl said she was Italian. Maybe it just made her happy. Maybe she thought she had missed some-

12

thing somewhere. She was just a bad idea, that's all. But she'd be gone and she was just paying him back for the fights and for being on the skids in a town where she didn't know anybody. Somebody had to pay for that offense. And he didn't mind, if it gave her a lift. It could be a gift he gave her.

2

THERE WERE PLENTY of edifying stories about the Oaxaca prisión. As many as there were parts of the body to get interested in. They began, once you told them, to have the appeal of dirty limericks. Each one was worse than the one before, but you kept listening indefinitely because of the pacing. There was the one about the American jockey with the big crank who fucked every whore that stumbled up the road from Animas Trujano, and came down eventually with a burning that made his testicles swell up and burst before a doctor could get inside. There was the one Sonny told him on his first visitor's day about the kid from Beloit with an earache who died in two hours when whatever it was in his ear made connection with his brain. People committed suicide with crochet needles. The *mayores* in the "F" barracks beheaded their boyfriends and left them in their beds for days. But the story that interested Quinn was the Austrian woman whose husband was doing years for holding ten Bolivian aspirins on a DC-3 bound for Cancun. The man was an appliance-store owner and wasn't healthy, and his wife flew from Vienna and visited him every day. And every day the matrons in the women's precinct submitted her to the most intimate personal searches. And after a while, Sonny said, the woman began to come twice a day, in the morning and during siesta, when the matrons had more time, and then more often, until eventually the matrons got bored and wouldn't search her unless she paid them. Otherwise they would pass her through to her husband. And the woman had long ago stopped being interested in him. It demonstrated, he thought, the way people adapted to circumstances when the circumstances went out of control. And it was in the spirit of things in Mexico. Mexico was like Vietnam or L.A., only more disappointing—a great trivial abundance of crap the chief effect of which wasn't variety but sameness. And since you couldn't remember the particulars from one day to the next, you couldn't remember what to avoid and control. And the only consolation finally was that you didn't have any stake in it, and Quinn didn't figure to be around long enough to earn one.

＊

Bernhardt drove the car intently, as though something was troubling him. They were out near the prisión on the American Highway driving too fast in Bernhardt's Mercedes. The morning had developed a painful opaline glare, and out behind, Oaxaca had scaled back flat in the distance, a matte plate of jacarandas and palmeras and square-roofed casitas and the pale double corona of the Santo Domingo Cathedral, the clear dreamy Mexican air diminishing everything. Mexican cities at a distance, Quinn believed, gave you a different illusion from American cities. They looked like dream oases, whereas American cities looked like disassembled nightmares, but the facts were reversed and American cities were better places when you got there.

"Last night we have a large cocaine interception at the airport," Bernhardt said. He looked concerned, as though the news disappointed him. "A shooting. One man, an American serviceman, is shot thirty times. The police even shoot each other in the excitement." Bernhardt stared straight ahead, his hands firmly on top of the steering wheel.

They were well out of the city now on the broad reach of flat highway. It was precisely what he wanted to stay clear of, the

15

periphery of things out of control. That was trouble. You had to stay center-on. There were a lot of second-class buses wallowing in the other way, old Flxibles with school coaches slop-painted red and white, jostling to pieces. And there were Indians lining the dusty roadside toward town. The Indians all walked with the same jaunty gait that made them look ambitious. "In Mexico," Bernhardt continued, "to obey the law is always to avoid it. If police are shot, then guerrillas are accused. Then the law comes to every place. And if guerrillas are accused, then there are more guerrillas to locate." He glanced at the Indians the car was passing. "Many people don't know they're guerrillas before the police say so. But they begin to act that way as soon as they find out." Bernhardt shrugged.

"That's real tough," Quinn said.

"Perhaps it won't matter to you now," Bernhardt said confidently. "Your wife arrives this afternoon?"

"That's the plan," Quinn said.

"And she will have everything?"

Bernhardt meant the money. "She'll have it."

"Then it will be smooth," Bernhardt said.

"That's what I want," Quinn said. "No spectacles."

When Rae had split he had started doing what they used to call winter camping. Finnish lunacy. He had driven in the Scout north of Antrim on the fifteenth of January, built a basswood platform for his tent, and begun to concentrate attention on the Ojibwas. He drove the corduroy roads and the pine slashes with his .336 across his lap and a chambered round, until he saw their cars, bricked down in the trunk, snugged in with dead falls across the hoods, old rusted Nashes and Studebaker trucks with the headlights blacked. He'd drive out at midnight with his lights off, secure the road with the Scout, and snowshoe up, following their narrow trail until he could hear voices. Then he'd circle out so that he came down on them from deeper in the woods where they weren't expecting anything. He had perfected the ability to travel silently, and so he would catch them stark in his seal beam

16

over a doe, smoking dope and stashing the sawed parts in black garbage bags to sled back to the cars. The Ojibwas called it high-speed beef, and it was a trick to plank a salt lick in a forked tree and let the deer work it through until they were leaning in to get at the last wafer crust when the larch stakes that formed a funnel to the salt caught them behind the neck and held them until the Ojibwas arrived in the trucks at night with their chain saws and cruiser axes. Sometimes the deer would freeze to death, and sometimes they'd rupture the big artery in their necks from bucking. But mostly they'd stand still and breathe until the men came softly up with their flashlights, saws, and garbage bags and cut their throats and bled them while the men sat and rolled a joint and waited for the carcasses to drain out. He caught twenty Indians the first month and the word began to spread around. He'd put the cuffs on them and walk them out to the road, set them in the back of the Scout, then drive the deer to the county locker and the Ojibwas to the Federal Marshall in Traverse City who fined them a hundred and turned them loose. He caught the same men again and again, and it got to be a joke. But he had the time, and he couldn't sleep two straight hours in the tent, and the Ojibwas never hassled, and there wasn't anything else to do until spring.

❋

The terrain now was high-mountain cordillera, pleated and folded into a long blind valley of brown unclassified earth turning chalk green downrange and curling toward the higher peaks like sandpaper. Once in a while, you could make out a red tower pricked above the palm plats in the tiny distant pueblos, but the land itself was degraded and upended. It was not the kind of landscape he liked. Not a complex landscape. The light was too clear and unvarying. In the States these mountains would have names, but here the sense of permanence was expressed differently, by an anonymity that made you aware of seeing only half a mountain, as if the other side could all be painted orange.

The people on the road were all Zapotecs carrying bound wool-ens and water tins into the mercado. Now and then a group of children danced at the edge of the road dangling iguanas on strings. The iguanas stroked slowly in the air while the children flailed them at the cars, but all Quinn could hear, fading, were cries that sounded like "good-bye, good-bye."

"If he had not signed a confession," Bernhardt said, "it would be easier now." He cleared his throat. "If he was braver."

"He wouldn't be our boy then," Quinn said. Something about Sonny's name made Bernhardt uncomfortable. He never spoke it. "So what do you do with a fucking iguana?" He looked back at the children traipsing away from the road toward a bombed-out adobe with no roof. It was never verifiable if most Mexican houses were half finished or half torn down.

"Set them loose," Bernhardt said authoritatively. He paused a moment. "Sometimes I buy one." He smiled in a comradely way. "And then I set it loose down the carretera. What could I do with it?"

Quinn faced the road again. "Let 'em keep it," he said. "Just pay off."

"They don't want iguanas." Bernhardt shook his head. "They are a nuisance. Why would they want them more than you do?"

Bernhardt was the Mexican lawyer he had paid to get Rae's brother out of the prisión. He had gotten on to Bernhardt through the consulate, who said Bernhardt had had success with American druggies, had reliable principles, and wasn't cheap. Bernhardt liked Americans and smiled a lot and seemed to have good connections with the administración de justicia. He was the best you could do. He reminded Quinn of the U.S.I.A. officers he had seen in the war, expensive suits, slightly balding, and a positive temperance that made you want to trust him. At best he figured Bernhardt wasn't bored enough to get involved if there wasn't a chance to buy Sonny out.

Bernhardt said he had a judge ready in two nights to execute a document of release for ten thousand dollars, and Rae was bringing cash on Mexicana in the afternoon. Bernhardt wanted to know nothing about money until the moment he needed it, and today they were simply making the drive as though nothing was going down, to let Sonny know he was leaving. If the human flow changed or if an insider got down in his Super Plenamins and smokes, word moved that a release was coming and everybody lined up for a handout. But if the release went off fast only the alcaide had to be paid, and that was it. It was going to be necessary to purchase the official document of release in the afternoon, and then get Rae, which was what Quinn was waiting for and the only stake he figured he had in anything.

Ahead, the army had arranged a new checkpoint on both sides of the road, with two sandbagged M-60s and plenty of help. Bernhardt stopped back of the barricade, showed his driver's license and his prisión card, and was passed through. The soldier looked at Quinn through the window but didn't check.

Beyond the barricade on the opposite shoulder a line of second-class buses waited in the dust to be inspected, swagged to the side with passengers going to market day tomorrow, bundles and baskets piled on top and all the greasy windows filled with attentionless Zapotec faces, staring out at the highway. The soldiers were making everyone in the first bus stand out and haul their belongings off the top-carry and open them. More soldiers watched from under the plank hut while the searchers cruised through the Indian passengers, pointing at bundles and yelling to make the women raise their dresses while the men stood awkwardly with their arms up. Quinn thought about Rae having to raise her skirt for soldiers. It wasn't anything she couldn't handle. In the waiting buses people were dropping fruit peels out the windows, and as the car eased down the line a pig's face peered out a window all alone.

"Pistols and explosivos," Bernhardt said very professionally. He steered casually along the row of buses without watching the searches. "Storms come, and birds can't fly to the sea, you know?" He smiled.

Quinn stared at the pig's impudent face. "Do they find any?"

"No," Bernhardt said confidently. "But they arrest for appearances. In United States, people respect money. But in Mexico, only *soldiers*. Tuesday you see nothing here. Last night an interception and today there are soldiers. Things could become difficult."

"I'll just count on you to stay clear of those difficulties."

"I hope it is possible," Bernhardt said.

Back in the line a red Dodge van was waiting for inspection. It had good tires and a gold university door seal. Inside were three rows of American college girls all talking at once and looking out the dusty windows at the front of the line. The driver was a Mexican tired of putting up with horseshit. He wasn't going to get fucked, and he wanted out of the sun. Quinn watched the girls go by. He wondered which ones would have to pull down their jeans for the soldiers and what they would tell whoever was paying for the trip. It was going to be an adventure.

"It can quickly become a time for responsible laws now," Bernhardt said and shook his head gravely. Bernhardt had big square incisors that were always moist. But he didn't show them now. "Mordida is a source of irritation," he said. "Like guerrillas. You do not have guerrillas in the United States. You are lucky."

"We live right, I guess," Quinn said, watching the valleyscape open like a fan.

"Perhaps one day. American cities invite it," Bernhardt said significantly.

"I'm in the here and now," Quinn said. "I can't worry about that."

Bernhardt looked at him seriously. "But you are in *this* now, Mr. Quinn. So you should know it intimately." Bernhardt glanced at the mirror and at the highway narrowing into the desert. Bernhardt liked heavy-duty comparisons, and he wasn't stupid about it, but some just didn't hold your attention as well as others. Bernhardt could make you impatient. "A man wants to give his wife a life so pleasing nothing in it wouldn't remind her of him. You see." Bernhardt looked at him seriously. "Is that not right?"

"It beats me." It was the orthodox lie Mexican men told themselves to make themselves feel like gods on earth. It was shabby, but everybody believed it.

"It is true," Bernhardt said firmly and drew a breath. "But the guerrillas are like a man whose wife fucks everybody but him and there's nothing he can do. He never pleases. He *is* never pleased. So he robs banks, shoots soldiers, blows up, sells narco, disparages everything. And everyone is *dis*pleased. And if your wife's brother traffics narco then he is like a guerrilla, an irritation, and people do not want to do a favor for him." Bernhardt turned and watched the highway glide by with satisfaction.

"Love's a hardship, right?" Quinn said.

Bernhardt looked at him as if they understood one another perfectly. "Exactly," he said, pleased. "It smells always of extinction."

"It's a sweet smell, though, isn't it?" Quinn said.

"Ahh," Bernhardt said, and smiled to show his incisors. "It *is* a sweet smell. There's nothing like it. But it is extinction just the same."

In a different setup, he thought he might've found a way to like Bernhardt, only the setup didn't include that now. Intimacy just made things hard to see, and he wanted things kept highly visible at all times.

✳

Animas Trujano centered on a low dry spot of highway with the big state prisión segregated above it by a long sandstone fault that gave the town the appearance of having been toppled off a more necessary layer of the earth. The village was a randy collection of tan and aquamarine thatch huts built along a mud alley that retailed whores and mescal to the prison, and a Zapotec herb market built under a long twig awning where the Indians bought Sidra and traded peyote buttons. Plenty of times he had seen moms and dads from Illinois standing out in the dirt alleys in their clean pastel suits and summer dresses, holding care parcels in both arms while the whores taunted them from the doorways of the little one-room chozas. Sometimes one of the smiling moms waved as if she saw something she recognized in his wide American face. But mostly they just stared up the highway in amazement as their cab left, as if they had been dropped backward into the worst dream they'd ever dreamed. Both his parents were dead, and thinking about the people lost on the streets of Animas Trujano made his situation seem worse, and he wanted to keep his spirits up, and the way to do that was not to see yourself as anything but yourself.

The prisión was a rhomboid made out of yellow sandstone behind a tall chain fence. There were metal guard turrets and gimbal lights at each corner and guards were conspicuous behind the windows and on the walls. From the highway approaching Animas Trujano you could see a high, red safe-box building inside with long low buildings connected like spokes. On top of the safe-box was a transmitter tower with a red slogan light, and beside it a copter pad slash-marked H. It was the most single-minded piece of construction he had ever seen, and from outside it was inconceivable that men were in it and that more men got put in it every day. It would refute something basic in you, Quinn thought, to be put inside. And so of course there wouldn't be any extremes beyond consideration to getting yourself out.

In Animas Trujano the whores weren't up yet. Portieres hung over their entries, though the doors to the mescalerías had been opened and green candles were already twitching inside. There were no moms and dads today and the town seemed inert and passed over. A Zapotec boy riding a bicycle flocked with wads of white cotton rode up the street against the direction of the car, followed by a dog, and there was a group of men standing beside an old green Impala that had crapped out in the middle of the street. Their heads were under the hood, and one pair of legs sprouted out into the strong sunlight. The boy seemed to be riding away from them.

"Mexican men either work on their cars or piss," Quinn said as the Chevy came up.

Bernhardt didn't answer. He took a black pistol from under his

22

jacket and put it in a space beneath the dash. Bernhardt had on a beige Italian suit, something, Quinn thought, you'd have to go a long way for. It made its own statement. "Maybe you should carry a gun," Bernhardt said. The boy on the bicycle waved as he pedaled past. "If you smell extinction," Bernhardt said appraisingly, "it maybe comes closer to you."

"I can't smell it," Quinn said.

"But you do." Bernhardt looked at him. "You are alone, that is detestable. Your wife is making you nervous now. So it scares you somehow, maybe."

"Not me," he said and looked at Bernhardt. "I was in the war. I don't get scared anymore. It's my big problem."

"Then you are lucky," Bernhardt said. He made the turn toward the prisión. He was silent for a moment. "Too many things scare me anymore. Too many things are to be afraid of."

"You're all loaded up though," Quinn said, pointing toward the gun. "Just stay between me and them."

"You may need to be close, though, before we're finished." Bernhardt attended the road carefully as it approached the fenced perimeter of the prison. There were soldiers and army police standing in groups on the inside of the fence and a brand new APC in front of the main gate with another sixty caliber podded on a truck bed. The soldiers stared at the car casually as if it made an uninteresting noise they had nothing better to do than identify.

"Just lay it all out for me so I can see it," Quinn said. He felt aggressive all at once. The prison made him alert, and that was the way he wanted to stay, alert to everything. "I like to be able to see everything when I do it."

"Maybe it will all please you," Bernhardt said.

Quinn glanced out at the yellow stone wall of the prison. It was long enough that at any one location you had no sense of there being an end to it. "I'd like to be pleased," he said. "It would be a real fucking experience."

3

IN VIETNAM Quinn had made a minor science of light-study. Light made all the difference in the way you performed and how you made out, since everything was a matter of seeing and not seeing. The right distribution of eastern grey and composite green on the surface of an empty paddy and a line of coconut palms could give you a loop, and for a special celestial moment you wouldn't be there at all, but be out of it, in an evening's haze of beach on Lake Michigan with teals like flecks of grey space skittering down the flyway toward Indiana, and the entire day would back up sweetly against a heavy wash of night air. And you could put it away then, ease your eyes, and wander outside another moment and join the world before the landscape began to function again as a war zone.

Mexicans all had faith that rooms needed lights, though they didn't have a systematic canon for where they went. Preference was for a single flo-ring bracketed midceiling, giving off just enough radiance to taint the air with an ugly graininess that seemed to hold bad smells, but wasn't quite good enough to see by. The effect in all cases was of no light, though there was always the illusion of light that made you look too hard at everything, and at the end of any day made your eyes smart and water from wanting to see better than you could ever see. It made you feel dirty in a way that wouldn't clean. It made all the daylight prospects seem jeopardized.

The visiting room had a poor light. The space was a long cafeteria, twenty-five by forty, inside one of the low pavilions chained to the administración safe-box. There had been a row of high casements down the long walls, but they had been bricked and florings installed. Quinn thought it might have been usable once, but it gave you a sharp retinal pressure that made you unsure moment to moment if you could distinguish correct figure from absolute ground. And he liked to be surer than that.

They had to wait for Sonny. The cafeteria was cool and quiet. There were patches of seepage on the concrete and armies of moyote beetles crawling out of the wall cracks, heading for the seepage so they could get in it and get on their backs and drown. The air had the thick sweet smell of burned cinnamon, and there were two brown-uniformed guards at either end with long rifles, watching an American prisoner whispering intensely to a woman across one of the long tables. He hated the room. It smelled like piss-stink Michigan grade-school cafeterias that made you gutsick and think life was shitty. The room was full of flies, though they didn't seem to bother Bernhardt. He was captured by the woman the American prisoner was talking to.

Sonny was let in the yellow metal door at the end of the cafeteria. The guard halted him, put his rifle against the wall, and patted Sonny down while Sonny stared into the room and smiled, his long fingers sensing the new air.

Sonny had been good hoops. He was six three and soft-palmed and ball smart, and at a distance he didn't look like somebody muling Baranquilla cocaine through Mexico into San Diego. He had once scored 100 points in a high-school game in New Rochelle, which was a state record, and when Quinn showed up a month ago, he looked like he could still do it, though he didn't look that good anymore. He had gone to J.C. and quit to play pro, then gotten waived and wound up playing in Sweden for two hundred dollars a game. He had come back in a year with a Benzedrine problem and a Swedish wife and begun playing I. leagues in L.A. and got into the business of delivering animal tranquilizers to the dog tracks in Tijuana for fixed rates. He was just starting to move lorazepam when Quinn had moved with Rae to Seal Beach two years ago, and even then muling didn't seem like a job you'd retire from. Sonny had floating, graceful arms and pale eyes that faked his moves and a way of walking toes-in that made you think he wouldn't go anyplace very fast, which was wrong. He had dropped thirty pounds in a month, his complexion had grown speed bumps, his eyes had gotten wide, and he had begun to tie his hair in a ponytail. He looked to Quinn like a freak, somebody you wouldn't stop for on the on-ramp.

Sonny smiled as he sat down. "Fucking flies, man. Carry you off."

Quinn looked down at the guards. "We're set now," he said in a whisper.

Sonny looked at Bernhardt and back as if he hadn't heard something correctly. His eyes narrowed alertly. Quinn shoved across the paper sack with Sonny's Allowable Personals—toothpaste, Super Plenamins, Lomotils, and a week-old copy of the *Houston Chronicle*. The guard who had passed Sonny in was staring at the paper sack, as if he thought it might contain something wrong. "Make this look right, please," Quinn said. "People are watching."

"When?" Sonny said softly. He looked inside the sack and made noise with it. His pupils were too dilated. They looked like fresh fish eyes, but his face was still controlled.

"Two days, three days," Quinn said. It irritated him to have Sonny show up loaded. "It'd help if you'd stay straight for just a fucking day or so."

Sonny rearranged himself on his stool and squared his shoulders. He laced his large hands on the table and bent forward. "Sure," he said and blinked rapidly. "No problem there." He looked at Bernhardt and then alertly back at Quinn and smiled.

26

This was killed-time starting now, and Quinn wanted out, but it was too fast. Short visits meant special things to the guards. "Where's Rae?" Sonny said.

"In the air. She'll be here."

"You two gonna patch your act up?" Sonny said and tried to extend the smile into a leer.

He wanted to stay cool. He wanted it right so Sonny could get out. But he didn't want to take shit. "That's none of your business," he said.

Sonny blinked again and forced his hands together as though he was trying to hold himself in on the center of something imaginary. The muscles in his arms kept seizing and relaxing. He was freaked, but that was his own problem. "I'm just a little wiped, you know? I did some crystal." He grinned and looked up at both of them apologetically. "It's like a strain, you know, in here."

"You bet," Quinn said.

The first time he met Sonny, Sonny was playing I. leagues in San Bernardino against some black noncoms from Victorville. Sonny was twenty-six and had some moves left. He was controlled and knew where the ball was when he didn't have it. Quinn had driven out after a day hunting fitter's work up the Catalina Channel. Rae was answering crisis phone calls and he was ready to get out of the basin and into something less weird. Sonny's team folded halfway and he let it slide in the last quarter, and when the game was over they drove in Sonny's yellow Cadillac back to San Pedro to a Japanese restaurant where Sonny knew people. At the table Sonny drank a beer and relaxed and studied his hands as if they were instruments he admired but couldn't quite figure out. "I could do that, you know, every day, twice a day. You know what I mean?" He looked up at Quinn confidently in the glassy bar-darkness. He turned his hand over, palm up. "But then where do I make a buck, you know?" His eyebrows twitched and he smiled. Quinn rubbed the beer glass around in his hands. He'd been digging up fitter's work and he hadn't thought anything about where Sonny was going to make a buck. "Sports is for kids, you know how that goes? Kids and niggers." He bit at his lip. "Sweden, I could dex up, shave six to make spread, and waltz out loaded. But that's not sports, Harry." He looked up. "That's business. I might as well be in the fucking record business. I'm getting old in this sports shit." He looked innocent, as if he were the first human to apply the truth of the world to his own private case. In a week he was trunking lorazepam to Tijuana, and Quinn didn't see much of him anymore, and in two months he and Rae had split east.

Down the room, the other American, a skinny boy with a clean T-shirt that read "Try God," was mumbling to the woman who had sunk down on her stool, letting the boy work her under the table with his foot. It seemed to interest Bernhardt.

"I got a card from Kirsten today," Sonny said and looked up respectfully. "She said if you were down here, Harry, she wasn't going to worry about me. She thinks you're smart because you were in Nam. You know?"

"Great," Quinn said. Kirsten had split when Sonny started muling. She had driven his Cadillac to the L.A. airport and flown to Uppsala and didn't tell Sonny where his car was for a month, and Sonny couldn't call the police because the trunk was full of lorazepam. She wasn't stupid, and Sonny knew it. And he knew he was. And that was why he was staying so mad about it.

"She's a cunt, you know?" Sonny said. He still seemed glad.

"You need anything else?" Quinn said. Enough time was by now for dress-up. He wanted outside. Sonny made him weakstomached.

"How're the Tigers?" Sonny looked at both of them as if he wasn't sure which one would answer. He seemed suddenly nervous, and squeezed his hands together harder. His breath smelled impure.

"Read it." Quinn shoved back the bag with the *Houston Chronicle* in it. Sonny's breath was making his saliva ropy.

Sonny began glancing at Bernhardt off and on. "I like the Tigers," he said. Bernhardt was still interested in the whore and not paying strict attention. He was just along for the ride this time, a public appearance. "Look," Sonny said indecisively. He stared back at Quinn. Sonny's face was pathetic, and he suddenly exhaled a lot of bad air all at once. "There was a guy here today." He kept staring at Quinn as if the words meant less if you didn't acknowledge them.

Bernhardt's attention settled back onto Sonny's face and he looked at Sonny oddly. Sonny opened his fingers deliberately on the tabletop and breathed in deeply.

"What's *that* mean?" Quinn said.

"An L.A. guy," Sonny said softly. He looked down. "It's fucked up."

"What kind of fucked up?" Quinn said. It surprised him, but there was a sense he wasn't hearing it right. He didn't want to raise his voice, that wouldn't be the way, except he wanted to hear it right. He felt muscles in his arm crawl.

"What are you talking about?" Bernhardt said patiently.

Sonny looked at Bernhardt, then back at his hands as if Bernhardt were talking about his hands. "They think I skimmed the stuff," he said meekly.

Quinn sat back on his stool and looked at the whore behind Sonny. He could see the backs of her calves where she had the stool straddled like a seesaw. Her toes were holding the concrete to keep the kid in the T-shirt from prying her off onto the floor. The kid's eyes were darting and his mouth had a frozen look of purpose. He was trying to reach something inside her that no one had ever reached before.

"They think what?" Quinn said.

"They think he makes the deal and lets himself be arrested," Bernhardt said calmly. He was staring at Sonny bemused. He ran his thumb down his jawline, then leaned on it.

"That's crazy, isn't it? Isn't that fucking crazy?" Quinn looked at Sonny hopefully. "You didn't to that, did you?"

Sonny tried to look insulted. "No way," he said. "I'm mules.

That's it." He started to raise his hands off the tabletop, then set them down again.

"That's crazy," Quinn said to Bernhardt.

"It is not impossible," Bernhardt said calmy and adjusted his glasses. Something in Sonny's face seemed to interest him, as though all his features had become more complicated. "It's happened before," he said. "Though not to my client."

"In here?" Quinn said. "To want to get in here?"

"One can arrange to get out," Bernhardt said. He raised his eyebrows. The muscles of his jaw rose beneath his cheeks.

Sonny looked at Bernhardt and Quinn quickly as if things were going wacko now. He made his ponytail swing. "No way," he said. "I don't own insides."

Quinn didn't like the edge in Sonny's voice. He couldn't figure out what was causing it and he didn't like that. "Are you fucking on me, Sonny?" he said.

Sonny's face got pale. "Look man," Sonny said, "don't bullshit me now."

He was pissed all at once, but under wraps. He didn't want to go in next. "I'm not shitting *you*. Why should I shit you? I'm down here to get you fucking out of this shit hole, you douche bag, and all of a sudden you don't sound right. You understand what I mean? You don't sound right to me. And I don't have a plan for that." He wanted to hear something to make sense or he was going to pack everything in the minute Rae got off the plane.

"Who is the man?" Bernhardt said intently, leaning forward.

Sonny breathed deeply and closed his hands around the paper sack as if it contained all his hopes and he was having to give it up. "A spade," he said and breathed again very deeply. "Deats. A guy named Deats."

"Who does he work for?" Bernhardt said.

"L.A. people. I don't know them. I've seen him before at the Lakers' games, you know. He's a big player."

"So is he a pal of yours?" Quinn said.

"I don't know him." Sonny shook his head in a bewildered way. "He's inside. I'm not inside."

"What did he say to you?" Bernhardt asked. He was being methodical now.

Sonny gripped the neck of the sack and licked his lips. "That he wanted the stuff."

"Why does he think *you* took it?" Quinn said.

"He said the police only took two pounds off me, and he paid for four." Sonny looked across at Bernhardt.

"What did you pick up?" Bernhardt said deliberately. "How many kilograms?"

Sonny shook his head. "I just pick up packages. I don't weigh it. Weighing's their business. I left the money in my hotel room, took a walk on the zócalo, and when I came back there were two packages on the bed. That's what the federales got."

Quinn looked at Bernhardt. "They must've copped it on him, right? Say that's right."

Bernhardt pushed out his lower lip and studied Sonny. "If it goes, it goes high up," he said. "For the police there is more money in doing things correctly." He smacked his lips and looked at Sonny matter-of-factly. "Do you have it?" he said.

Whatever Sonny had popped on had burned off in sixty seconds. His face was gaunt and his eyes looked ruined. He looked to Quinn like somebody who'd run a long way without stopping, for the first time in his life. "No," he said almost silently and shook his head.

"And you don't know who anybody is?" Quinn said.

"L.A. people," Sonny said softly. "I know a guy in L.A. He pays me. It comes through Mexico because it's safer than straight up. But I don't meet anybody down here. I just mule." He looked up pitiably. "I'm not smart enough. You understand?"

"How much time did he give you?" Bernhardt said, interrupted by some low moaning coming from the whore on the stool. Bernhardt turned to look at her.

"He didn't say." Sonny stared at Bernhardt expressionless,

waiting for his attention to come back. He was wanting a miracle. Quinn knew the look, though he didn't care about it on Sonny. His face just wasn't useful to what he felt.

"You fucking putz," he said and sighed. He wanted to let Sonny take it all down. But there wasn't even any way for that now. He was in too far.

Sonny looked like he might cry. "It's a setup," he said. "What am I supposed to do?"

"Who's supposed to be set up?" Quinn said. "You? Are you worth setting up, asshole?"

"I don't know," Sonny said and shook his head pathetically.

Bernhardt stood up. The whore had finished making noise and was sitting straight on her stool, fanning her cheeks with her hand. The boy looked radiant. The room was quiet except for the fan at the end, and the sound of the guards' feet scuffing. "Try to stay tranquilo," Bernhardt said courteously.

Sonny opened his mouth to speak, but Bernhardt wasn't listening. He had started toward the exit.

"What's happening?" Sonny said. He seemed amazed.

"You fucked this up," Quinn said. "This was slick, and now it's fucked up."

"What're you going to do?" Sonny said.

"Guess," Quinn said.

Sonny looked pathetic again. "When's Rae coming?" he said.

Bernhardt was already out the door. "Don't think about her," Quinn said. "Just pretend she doesn't exist."

"This is dumb," Sonny said. "Jesus this is so goddamned dumb."

"Is that right?" Quinn said. "You're a fucking genius, man. I don't know how you ever got in here." He walked down between the rows of tables toward the blank wall where the exit was.

4

THE HIGH MOUNTAIN on the west valleyside had lost the sun
and blackened down to the color of green without light. In the
winter, chaparral fires blossomed in the steep inclines and defiles,
hanging a mask of haze to the terminus of the valley. The fire
burned for weeks, and people stopped noticing it, and after a
while the smoke just became part of the landscape. It was, Quinn
thought, the way you got yourself used to everything. It was like
imagination, and then it was the way things were. And then you
couldn't tell the difference.

"So how do we find this guy?" he said. Rae would be here
too soon and things weren't falling out just right.

"It won't be difficult." Bernhardt adjusted his glasses with his
thumb and fingers, then squinted over the steering wheel toward
Monte Albán, clear in the open distance west, where there were
still morning light windows on the precipices. Bernhardt was driving fast. "What would your wife's brother do for money?" he said
calmly.

"Nothing that big," Quinn said. "He couldn't lay off that much."

"He could mail it to an apartado in the States, a dummy."
Bernhardt seemed to enjoy the speculation.

"He's too little."

"A great deal of trouble can be caused by little liars. You understand?" Bernhardt looked at him appraisingly.

"No way," he said. "He doesn't have a big imagination."

Bernhardt fastened his eyes back on the highway. "Then we will have to impress the other man," he said. "Mr. Deats. I will have to find a way to do that."

"What happens meantime?" His mind was on Rae. It was too late to call her in Texas. She'd be out of the motel already.

"We will purchase the document of release," Bernhardt said evenly. "I will go on with the arrangements to the judge. You will meet your wife. Things will go as we planned them. We can't *worry* about Mr. Deats. It is a delicate situation."

They were approaching the army spec station from the opposite direction. More buses sat queued on the dusty shoulder wheezing smoke. Soldiers were busy on top of the lead coach throwing boxes and bundles on the ground while the Indians stood passively with their arms over their heads. The red travel van that had been in the queue before was parked beside the station hut with all its windows broken and its seats pulled out. None of the girls was around anymore. They were Americans, but there was nothing he could do for them, and it gave him a cold bone feeling to wonder where they were and what they were getting to look at next.

Bernhardt pulled out around the buses to center highway, idled to the barricade, showed his license, and was passed.

"In twenty years," he said when he had gained speed, "Mexico will be governed by defectives, the children of these people." He motioned backward toward the campesinos standing in the dirt for search. There was a profound sympathy that rivaled distaste in his voice. But it was tone and no substance. "They are fed on garbage. And one day nothing will please them anymore." He reached under the dash, removed the pistol, and put it back under his coat. "And then you and I will have a big problem."

"It doesn't worry me much." Quinn said. He thought about his own pistol in the bungalow, and Bernhardt's advice to carry it. It wasn't smart.

"Why?" Bernhardt said and smiled, as though all the alternatives were amusing.

"Because if that time comes and I'm alive, I won't be right here."

"Where will you be?" Bernhardt said.

"Far away from here."

"One never knows," Bernhardt said, letting himself be distracted again by the mountains, visible only as a black mass in the west.

"Oh yeah," Quinn said. "One knows that. One knows that for sure."

He wondered precisely where, down the line, Bernhardt would bolt. He knew he would somewhere, and he wanted to anticipate it, so that when Bernhardt hit out, there'd be one more option left for himself and Rae. One was enough. He watched a white helicopter skimming the blue air to the east, out of hearing, its tail strung up as if a fine, invisible filament was hauling it on. It was nuts, he thought, to be tied to somebody, two counting Bernhardt, you had no feeling about, but who somehow made all the difference. That was the essence of the modern predicament. The guy who had it in for you was the guy you'd never seen. The one you loved was the one you couldn't be understood by. The one you paid to trust was the one you were sure would cut and run. The best you could think was maybe you'd get lucky, and come out with some skin left on.

5

HE HAD MET RAE at the dogs. He had been back from Vietnam eight months and through Pendleton, thinking all the time that the one lesson the war had taught was that everybody back in the world was lucky, and the best thing you could do the moment they turned you loose was push your luck on out and find some way to take a chance and some place to take it.

He had bought a Firebird off a sailor in Oceanside and drove it to Arizona, then down to Corpus Christi and across to Morgan City, Louisiana. In Morgan, the car dropped reverse and while he was waiting for parts he started taking seven-on, seven-offs for a pipe contractor supplying the hammer companies out on the Atchafalaya and Pigeon Bay as far out as Point au Fer. He had had a sense when he joined the marines that the country he was skying out of was a known locale, with a character that was exact and coordinate and that maintained a certain patterned feel. A thing you could get back with if you had a reason. But that patterned feel had gotten disrupted somehow, as though everything whole had separated a little inch, and he had dropped back in between things, to being on the periphery without a peripheral perspective. They weren't any war dreams of men you'd killed screaming underwater without sound. (He couldn't commit specific fears to memory.) But he felt alone without quite feeling bad, like being in the afterimage of a catastrophe, though he thought he'd gotten used to catastrophes all right without falling apart.

In Morgan he traded the Firebird and four thousand dollars for a Porsche, decided to hang in for the money, and moved out to company bunks in an Alamo Plaza painted company blue out Route 90. On his seven-off he liked driving up to Kenner to the dog track and playing cards in the bars in Evangeline Parish and working the women. He didn't have any plans. All the colleges he'd ever been in didn't teach him what he'd learned in two years out of the world, that once strangers you couldn't see started shooting guns at you and trying to set you on fire way up in the sky, plans didn't take you too far. And the only thing smart you could do was try to stay efficient and keep your private shit together. He'd picked up the tattoo in Hawaii. Good conduct was what kept you in the picture, kept ground underneath you instead of on top, and that was the only basic concept you could count on.

When he saw Rae she was standing in the bettors' pavilion under the grandstand, watching the TV monitor that had a dog race in progress. She was tall and elegant with long red hair, wore tight black jeans that cost some money, and a green halter that showed her breasts. She was holding a copy of Fourier's *New Industrial World* under her elbow and a wad of yellow win tickets in her hand, and she looked wrongly placed, which he guessed was the point.

He checked the old men in plaid suits and white socks who were watching the monitor, and the women wheelchair bettors cruising down the concourse in motorized chairs. He wanted to guess which one was paying her bills. His second dog hit, but when he came back holding his $4.80, Rae was still watching the monitor showing the pale pink racetrack with his winning number flashing at the bottom. The guys in plaid suits had all scattered toward the payoffs and the wheelchair women had gone to the refreshments. But she hadn't moved. And he suddenly liked the air. It had the stacked, cooled feeling of below zero ground, the nonplace where anything thinkable was possible if you didn't expect a long engagement. It was what the world left available.

He took one more look around. "You waiting for Johnny Carson?" he said.

Rae looked at him and at the four dollars in his hand as though he wasn't seriously there. She had on dark rouge and her eyes were flecked green. She was exotic looking, like she'd just come from someplace illegal, and she was speeding. That seemed like the right combination.

"What d'you think they do with the ones that don't win?" she said, and looked back at the suspended screen as though she'd asked the question to no one in particular, not even herself.

"Shoot 'em," he said quickly, and took another survey of the pavilion, to see if somebody was coming after her.

"I've got a candidate, then," she said flatly, "but he already left, I guess."

"You just read this crap between races?" he said. He didn't know who Fourier was, but he was betting he was somebody who started a revolution in Jamaica.

Rae smiled appealingly and snapped her head to sweep her long hair off her shoulders. "He doesn't know enough," she said, and sighed. "The guy who knows everything is the guy who runs the rabbit. He's in control of fate. You don't know him, do you?"

He figured enough time had gone by now. "I dont want to pry, but you haven't been to Mississippi, have you?" he said.

She didn't look at him. "Yeah, it's a shit hole," she said.

One of the wheelchair women was straining toward the TV monitors with a stack of green show tickets under her watchband, and her jaw swinging, unable to be still. It wanted to smile when there wasn't anything to smile about. He was nervous the woman had Rae in hock for her clothes.

"Well, since you liked it so much, how about let's go again?" he said in a hurry.

Rae frowned at the woman in the electric wheelchair. "There's a lot of geeks around here, aren't there?" she said.

Quinn had on new fawn whipcords and an eighty-dollar hand-made silk shirt from Charnet Street in Bangkok, and he guessed she had him down for a loser trying to get fucked free. But that was going to be her worry.

"You think I'm turned out, don't you?" Rae said, looking up at the monitor again.

"Of course not," he said. The wheelchair woman was buzzing toward them. She had a wrist watch on each arm, and they made him feel like his own time was getting short.

"I'm really a scientist doing research on assholes," Rae said and shook her hair out. "I thought this was the best place to find them, what do *you* think?"

"What about Mississippi?" he said and smiled at her. "I don't have all day."

Rae looked at him in a weary way that made her face burnt out. She knew he'd already figured something out and she was just trying to decide what difference it made if he was right and how seriously she was going to have to take him. She looked up at the monitor, where the track was empty and motionlessly pink, then back up the long line of payoff windows with green and yellow blinking lights signaling the high rollers with good tickets. "We'll just talk, right?" she said cruelly, and let her win tickets flutter away. "I can have my luggage sent on later."

✳

They spent the next six days in a roomette in Mississippi City, facing Route 90 and the Gulf. Rae had two ounces of Mexican hash, and Quinn had the best part of nine hundred dollars, and they stayed out on the shell beach every day until dark, then drove in to Biloxi to the bars. Late at night in the room they'd get loaded and drink beer and dance to Chicago radio until early in the morning when Quinn could get to sleep without pills.

Rae said she was a landscape painter from New York. She had spent six years after Brooklyn Academy living in Taos with a boy from New Rochelle who made adobe houses and sold hashish to skiers. She said she was thinking about opening a shop when he got busted and sent to Santa Fe, and she had come down to Tesuque to wait, and got a job caseworking on the Nambe pueblo and teaching grammar-school kids to paint mountain sunsets. She said casework was a lot like being in jail, except hotter, and she hated it, and after a year she got tired of being by herself and moved into Santa Fe with a bureau lawyer who was a Rosebud Sioux from Yale interested in politics and not too smart, but who had a big house and a Mercedes and wanted to marry a white woman. She said she got along with the lawyer until he decided he wanted her to have his baby, and hassled her so that she ended up having to treat him like any other fucked up Indian on her case list with obsessions about never dying, and she began drinking and taking too much mescaline and finally quit visiting the boy in prison, and thought about moving back to Long Island. But one morning she just left with a guy she'd met at a charity rodeo, another Indian, a better one, she said, a Ute named Frank Oliver from Lewiston, Washington, who was an ex-convict, a saddle bronc rider, and a car thief, who laughed all the time and had plenty of money and didn't care about being immortal if he didn't have to die right away.

Frank Oliver drove a big blue and silver Southwind that he'd stolen, with a painting of Mount Rainier on both sides and a two-stall horse trailer (a get-up she said they used to laugh about every day), and he pulled the trailer around the country to stock shows and rodeos, wherever he could ride broncs and strip cars for parts. The Southwind had a big stereo and red velour swivel chairs and indirect light, and she said the whole thing surprised her about herself, but she had discovered Cabet and spent one straight four-month period inside the RV, painting landscapes out the window, reading and getting stoned in the mornings with Frank, and riding through towns trying to draw a good mental picture of whatever she'd been doing for seven years and not been able to stay exactly current with. She said she just suddenly got frantic in Santa Fe and had to cut loose from everything responsible, so that it didn't matter if she lived in a trailer or a house or who she lived with, as long as there wasn't any trouble and there was some sense of pleasing variety. She said sometimes Frank would come in drunk at night and so banged up from horse falls he couldn't even laugh, and she'd have to get straight to drive the next day while he laid up and slept long enough to make entry wherever the next town was and get himself connected with whoever was stealing cars. And she said on those days, when Frank was asleep and she was driving, she figured out that what she was doing was simple craziness and nobody in his right mind would be doing it, but it was all she could bear to think about longer than a minute.

Rae said her brother was in Los Angeles playing Industrial leagues basketball and her father was a landscape painter in Bay Shore, and that she didn't have any plans. She said she could have stayed with Frank or not stayed with him, and that while it wasn't necessarily any good, it wasn't necessarily bad either. Until Frank broke his reins hand in a calf rope in Houston and had to lay off riding. She told Frank she would go to work painting street portraits if he'd buy her an easel and some brushes, and instead he had driven them to New Orleans and gotten in touch with an Italian he knew who was exclusively stealing Alfa Romeos and loading them on boats to Venezuela, and told her she didn't have to work and put her up in the Monteleone Hotel. Though after the first week he'd gotten busted, and when Rae bailed him out of the Orleans Parish jail she told him something would have to change or she was splitting, and he had taken her to the dog track and stood her under the TV monitor in the middle of the main pavilion and told her that when she got ready to, she could start making money the best way she could, using the Southwind out at the end of the parking lot under the row of palmettos.

She smiled at Quinn in the half-light and stretched her long arm up into the cool shadows. "I was resisting not being young anymore. I was almost thirty. It's textbook. It's my penance." She was just waiting to find the reason not to take him seriously, but she had a sweet unpretending elegance he felt at ease with, and she talked not because she thought it was important, but because they passed the time in an amusing way. "Maybe I'm a bum," she said. "I just missed being a hippie."

He could see the little pit fires on Ship Island twinkle in the night like stars. They didn't remind him of anything, and he was at ease for the first time he could remember. "*You* can't call yourself a bum," he said. "Somebody else has to do that. You don't get it both ways."

Rae sighed a long sigh. "But is that what you think about me?" she said, not interested in it. "You've been protecting our country's honor. You should be an authority."

"I don't know you well enough," he said, and ran his hand over her flat stomach.

"No judgments on the first date?"

"I'm not an authority on anything," he said. "That's all."

"That's nice," she said, and kissed him sweetly on the mouth. "Don't let me put any pressure on you. I don't want to do that. This'll be over soon enough."

She told him that when he saw her standing under the monitor she'd been there four hours holding the same win tickets, watching every race and the empty track in between, and trying not to get uptight, but hoping all the time something would come along to improve her prospects before the lights went out. She said turning her out was just Frank's way of saying good-bye, everybody had a way of saying good-bye, and if when Quinn showed up they'd have gone out and looked for the Southwind with the painting of Mount Rainier, it wouldn't have been there.

"Those little self-contained systems just get smaller," she said, when Quinn was almost asleep. "They're fine. But they don't tolerate enough. You know what I mean? You don't, do you?" He could hear her in a drowse. "They're like Frank. They make things simple. I thought I could get along with that. I should have figured it out a long time ago that I couldn't."

The Fourier she had was a loaner from the New Orleans Public Library, and she left it in a Tote-Sum in Mississippi City and

42

didn't ask to go back and get it when she found out it was gone.

He was drawn to her. She was his first serious business since he'd come back, and she made him feel hooked up, even if he hadn't planned on a permanent guest. He wasn't sure what exactly he was doing with her, but it didn't feel like the wrong thing, and it beat Route 90 in the Alamo Plaza rolling for beers, hustling fat coon-ass girls, then lurching back drunk at 5:00 A.M. by himself with no place to go but Seconal-land. Rae'd get stoned after midnight with the light on in the little pink hotel room and tell him there was something interesting about him from having been in the war. He didn't seem, she said, at all ready to kill anybody and loud noises didn't make him duck. He was like a doctor, she said, who cured exotic diseases and who had some of the disease left on him, but only enough to make her not want to split right away. Splitting, she said, had gotten to be a specialty.

After six days Quinn drove back to Morgan, checked out of the Alamo Plaza, rented a little railroad house on stilts outside the levee up Six Mile Palourde and moved Rae in, then went back running pipe to the rigs on Atchafalaya. Rae hit St. Vincent de Paul's for furniture, bought an easel, and sat out afternoons drawing from *National Geographics* and *Audubons* out of the Parish bookmobile, and playing the Eagles into the cypress swamps, stoned.

There was a feeling Louisiana was just another place for her, like Bay Shore or New Mexico, and she simply adapted right. But he felt like there was some hollow place in *him* where she made a feeling come at night. Whatever he wanted to do, it seemed like in her judgment she wanted to do it, though it was clear to him it didn't matter to her who she was with as long as she got adjusted for what she was doing moment to moment. She was locked in present time, he thought, and she was calm and deliberate as if she understood that, even understood the desperation to it, desperation she knew all about and could recognize but didn't need to acknowledge, as if it was obvious to anybody who knew her and perfectly natural and something to

43

smile about, even if what he felt was the same desperation, only for different reasons.

Sitting out on the high porch with the music, watching her row herself patiently, with long, graceful arms and a green paisley scarf on her head, out into the black water of the Palourde to sit and fish for crappies in the sunshine, he figured she made up what she needed as she went, the complicated parts included now. Nothing got by her. And she seemed older than he was, with a view of the world she had learned to put herself into with ease, and, if he wanted her to do it, could put him in, too, though that wasn't absolutely necessary to her survival, since she wasn't waiting for anything else to come along that hadn't already come once.

After three months with her he took papers as a fitter's helper and began taking extra days filling spots on the rigs when somebody was slow turning around. It started to make him feel dangerously *in* something to be in the house seven days, eating and sleeping all alone with her, listening to her mellowed-out music and sitting watching her paint from magazines slowly and calculatedly. Awake at 2:00 A.M. listening to the lizards on the porch and the mosquitoes zizzing through the dense blanket of air, he would start to drift away, and she would suddenly moan out in the darkness and flinch hard and hold him until he couldn't breathe. And he had to get out of the room and stand on the porch where the air was cooler and get calm. He thought with anybody sooner or later you got to an end point, one last event in a series of events at the end of which there was just a wall of empty air and things got invisible, and then you were in it with them, like it or not, and you had to make up whatever else came along. That was what Frank Oliver had figured out when he left her standing with a handful of win tickets. In the war you maintained your crucial distance from things and that kept you alive, and kept everything out in front of you and locatable. It was why Frank had his cars and his saddle broncs and his Southwind, and why he got scared the moment he even thought he might lose them. He could see all that and negotiate it. He probably hated to lose her. But he saw how much he was losing control *with* her, and he couldn't handle it. It was like losing track of a rule, not even that she wanted it lost, but just that she didn't need a rule herself. And mornings, when he would wake up in the bed, he'd be sweating and as far away from her as he could be, his shoulders and his fingers aching, his head full of noise. And he'd lie in the grey swamp light, feel her breathing, and wish he could move off on some other safer plane of existence, someplace maybe not too far, but far enough to be safe.

On the rig they told him that in L.A. if he could make the airplane factories and the Exxon rigs up the Catalina Channel and kept his name alive, something would pop open in a month. He had eight thousand in the Morgan Bank, and if he stayed four more months he could double it on layoffs, and if you were taking chances what you needed was money. But he thought he needed to make a move. If he was going to stay with Rae—and he wanted to—he needed to get someplace where there was a legitimate outside and where the outside risks were higher than the inside ones. Because where he was now all the risks were the kind you couldn't see, and those were the ones that scared him. It was his own doing and not hers, he knew. But everything was your own doing one way or another, and you had to live by yourself with the results at the end.

6

HE FELT FEVERISH for the first time now. His bowels had begun to quease and his mouth was sticky, and he had a sweat up. Sick was dangerous, he knew that. Sick never made you scared, just reluctant, and that was worse. Everybody in Vietnam had been sick, but the rhythm had geared down gradually, and the war had finally been run on sick time. People depended on each other according to sick intervals, watched each other with the expectation of diseased response. But in Mexico it was dangerous. It singled you out. Only assholes who drank water or ate candy off the urethane sheets on the street corners got sick. And he was on top of that. He had put a Halazone in every glass of water and considered every bite before he took it. The one thing you didn't want to be was sick when things began to happen, and right now he didn't quite have it.

Bernhardt had let him out in the Centro opposite the statue of Admiral Antonio Leon, facing the west, and drove off to check on Deats, whoever he was. Oaxaca was built to the medium municipal standard of small Mexican cities, two parks and a church, catty-cornered, with an open-air portal squaring everything. Americans drinking at the outdoor tables said you could see everyone in Oaxaca in a matter of an hour, and everyone you ever knew in a year. But that wasn't enough of an inducement. A group of women had gotten out of a yellow and green tour bus across the zócalo park and were setting up their aluminum easels on the eminence of the cathedral. They were crisp in the way they stood easel legs between the cobbles, as if they had pictured doing it every night for a month. They looked like Americans, and they looked anxious. They intended to paint the cathedral in the straight noon light, which was a mistake, he thought, but it was serious to them.

His stomach began to cramp vigorously, and he walked across the alameda and down Hidalgo to a pharmacy. It was wrong to be in town past noon. Bad light, rain, and then it got lonely, not like an American city, and he wanted to get up the hill to the bungalow and lie down. He bought a plaquette of Lomotils and took three, standing in the farmacia doorway. Bad customers. You took Lomotils furiously in Vietnam, and they shut you down eventually and made you melancholy and forgetful. After a while they were worse than being sick. But he thought with luck he'd be out before his insides collapsed. "Kill the body, the head dies." It was a joke then.

He walked back up Hidalgo toward where the streets changed names, to the cabstand. The streets changed names at the Centro and made the town hard to learn. He wanted to wash the prisión smell and the Italian girl off his skin before Rae showed up. And he needed to sleep, to let Sonny settle out. It would be raining in an hour, and he wanted out of the middle of things.

The Centro was crowded, and the streets were noisy and full of motorbike traffic. The air libres on the Portal were all open. Waiters stood in the arcades, snapping white napkins sullenly toward the few empty tables. Quinn walked out of the Portal and into the warm sunlight. There was a thick rain smell out of the park and the center of town felt too active with tourists and American hippies hanging with the Mexicans. There was a sense of anticipation he didn't like. The fountains were turned on. The Zapotec women were seated on the plaza plaiting their children's hair, and there were a lot of blue police at the perimeter of the park in their swaybacked hats and dirty ascots, waiting for something wrong to happen that they could stomp on. The second-class buses that had been out on the highway were arriving, clogging the arterial streets, with greasy faces still at the windows and soldiers asleep in the step wells. The wire mesh Christmas bells were strung all the way round the zócalo, and there were lights in the jacarandas, and a big silver tree stood riotously on top of the band kiosk. Mexicans thought Americans wanted it to be Christmas every day and they were happy to provide the illusion.

The American women who had set up their easels beside the cathedral were already in the Portal having coffees, sitting in the oily shade admiring their intentions. At the door to the cathedral two girls in white communion dresses waited to step through the high door. While he watched, a Mexican boy in a red T-shirt appeared at the wall of the cathedral. The boy stared at the easels for a moment and at the girls standing on the stone steps, then darted down the row of easels, kicking the third legs so that the easels were all flattened in ten seconds, the paints spilled over the stones, and the boy vanished back in the crowds down Busta-mante. One of the women in the Portal screamed, but most of them just sat still when they saw the easels go. It was efficient work, a nice symmetry. The women should've been able to tell, he thought, that precisely that event would take place. But they couldn't. It was what made them tourists. They looked and didn't see.

He read the American paper in the cab and tried to sit still so the Lomotil could work. Altitude had effects. One disease could imitate another. He pressed below his right floating rib. A swelling would mean hepatitis, but there was no swelling.

All the stories in the American news were published in the wrong syntax. U.S. TEAM WINS ISRAELI RIFLE SILVER. Below it was a photo of some American marksmen holding rifles and smiling in yarmulkes and nylon jackets. Another said ASSOCIATION OF TWINS INTERNATIONAL MEETS, and above it was a photo of some fat twins. There was a story about a grandmother in South Dakota stabbing a lion to death with a button hook inside her travel camper. The story didn't say how the lion had come inside the camper or why there was a lion around at all. Mexicans would understand it. Americans lived in an ocean-to-ocean freak show, and there was a good reason to be here where things were simple instead of up there where things were bent wrong. He checked for baseball scores in the back but there was only fútbol from the Federal District. He put his head back and closed his eyes and tried to let the pills work. Only assholes got sick. He couldn't be sick now.

✳

The bungalow didn't smell good. The moza was supposed to come in the morning to scrub the floor and launder the sheets, but it was clear she hadn't been there. The Italian girl's blue paisley underpants were lying in the doorway to the bedroom. The bed, in the shadows, was still torn up, the sheets half on the floor. He picked up the underwear and walked through the entry to the living room to open the mirador. Someone was in the living room.

"I can't see how you rate this nice place," the Negro said. He was standing at the picture window, and when he spoke he half turned and glanced out the window as if the best part of the bungalow was outside. Quinn got completely still. He wanted to be between the man and the bedroom, which led to the bathroom where the pistol was. He estimated eleven steps, no locks. "They've got me in some kind of bad shit bag." The Negro smiled and let his eyes come to Quinn. The television was on, but the sound was off. The room felt too small.

"I think you got the wrong address," Quinn said. He felt prepared to move. He knew who the man was. He didn't know if the man would know that.

"I want you to tell your boy to start doing me right," the Negro said, and sat down in the swivel chair. He looked at his fingernails as he talked.

49

Quinn thought four seconds to get under the tiles and have some competence with the pistol. A cramp fluttered at the bottom of his stomach. Not an urgent sign, but an urgent sign wasn't far back. A second man stepped out of the bedroom pointing a revolver at him. A Mexican, an older man in a pink rayon shirt and rheumy eyes who was taller than the Negro and was wearing a straw porkpie hat. Quinn looked back around at the Negro. " 'Fraid I don't get it," Quinn said. "Maybe you could just tell me who in the fuck you fellows are?"

The Negro took a joint from his shirt pocket, lit it, and watched Quinn through the smoke while he downed the toke.

"I know *you*," the Negro said in a constricted voice and smiled. "You been to Big Nam, got all kinds of good sense. You're down here getting your man out of the J." Deats held his hit as long as he could, his smile widening all the time. His face was khaki colored and smooth. He was thin and in his twenties and had on an expensive beige sweater and creased pants. He didn't look like anybody Sonny would get to know real well.

"Look." Quinn looked back at the Mexican holding the pistol. The Mexican hadn't made any noise. He was standing impassively in the bedroom door pointing the revolver. Quinn looked back at Deats hopefully. "I picked up a little dys," he said, "and I'm not in fighting shape right now."

Deats let his hit seep all the way out, delicately pinched off the red tip with his fingers, and put the joint back under his sweater. Deats had a piece, but you couldn't know where it was or how close to his hand, though the Mexican presented the first problem.

"Their water's got shit in it." Deats wiped his fingers together neatly and sniffed, then waited a moment. "Your man played bold down here," he said calmly, flicking ashes off his trouser crease. He didn't seem completely interested. "You know that?" He looked up smiling.

"He said he didn't," Quinn said.

Deats touched his nose again. "Uh-huh." He nodded patiently. "But he *did*. It don't matter what he *said*."

50

The dope made the room swampy and changed the light. Quinn was sweating again, and his toes felt slick. "I can't work with that," Quinn said. He balled the Italian girl's underpants in his fist. "That's not what I'm good at."

Deats smiled. "I know that," he said. He was a handsome boy with long, delicate fingers that he took nice care of.

"Look." He turned halfway toward the Mexican so he could keep them both in sight. "Maybe you could come back some other time." The Mexican stared at him as if he were a long way away from what was happening.

"We won't be too long," Deats said. He glanced at the TV. A small fat man with a painted-on mustache was standing beside a fat woman who was grinning and wringing her hands. The man was about to spin a big number wheel, and the fat woman appeared to have a lot of pain riding on the spin. The camera kept closing on her face, and her eyebrows twitched as if she could feel the pressure of the tiny screen.

The Mexican was behind him unexpectedly. He grabbed the hand with the Italian girl's underpants, pulled back swiftly, and tied it to the other one with a length of metal wire. Quinn let the underpants go. No resistance. He thought about the Italian girl having been in the room this morning. It seemed ridiculous.

Deats fidgeted with the armrest, his other hand holding a small silver pistol that looked like a cigarette lighter. "You can do your man a big favor," he said, calmly watching Quinn be tied up. The Mexican took his belt, looped his ankles, and knotted it back tight. The Mexican was breathing hard. "You can *tell* him for me," Deats said, "that I'm not in this fuckin' business to let assholes take me off like I was selling brooms. You understand that?" His mouth twitched and he suddenly seemed mad. It was just weirdness. Deats' eyes seemed to get much smaller and more finely focused.

Quinn wanted to keep his mind off his stomach. "Sure, I understand. Everything's great now," he said. He was having trouble keeping his balance. He thought he might fall backward.

"Speak to your man," Deats said calmly, and nodded at the Mexican. The Mexican whispered close to Quinn's ear, "Please kneel." Quinn bent over and the Mexican let him to the floor gently, face on the tiles. The floor began pushing the cramps back.

"And say what the fuck?" he asked, face down. He couldn't see Deats anymore, only his high-dollar alligator shoes, but he wanted to keep contact. "I told him if he had something you wanted, to turn it loose. He doesn't have the nuts to take you off."

The Mexican turned him over carefully so that he was lying on his tied hands looking at the corrugated fiber glass ceiling. It was a shitty place, a shittier place than he'd ever been in. The Mexican unbuttoned his shirt and pulled it open.

"Tell him he's a greedy boy," Deats said, staring down smiling. The little silver automatic was gone.

The Mexican began tampering with something in his own shirt pocket, not getting it out easily. "Maybe somebody else's taking you off," Quinn said. "Did you ever think of that?" You didn't look at the Mexican now. You kept your eyes on the green corrugation and talked to the ceiling.

"No," Deats said. His eyes had gone as swampy as the air. It was good dope. "My business just don't run that track, you understand?"

Quinn thought he could talk forever now. It was like the moment before anesthesia. "But Sonny can have you off. Right?"

Deats stood up out of the chair. The Mexican in the porkpie hat was ready with whatever he wanted to get, and waiting for Deats to give a sign. He could just see the Mexican's nose. Deats peered down at him. "Tell *him* what I tell *you*," Deats said. He walked across the room and turned the volume up on the TV. The Mexican had a small square plastic box, the kind trout flies came in. Deats stood in front of the TV and watched the Mexican oddly. He had his porkpie pushed back and he squeezed the lid off the box with this thumbnail, knelt, and delicately turned the contents out onto Quinn's chest. The Mexican had extremely thick fingernails, industrial fingernails, nails for turning screws. The man on the TV with the mustache was talking very fast in Spanish. He kept pointing to something off the screen and saying "grande." He kept reaching for the wheel as if he was going to spin it, then stopping and saying something to the fat woman that made her wring her hands harder and grin and flick her eyebrows and rise up on her toes in anticipation. The camera showed her toes. Quinn's heart began to whip up fast. "You don't look so hot," Deats said.

He thought he was going to have a cramp. The muscles up and down his stomach began organizing themselves into a unit, waiting for the scorpion to hit him. Quinn heard the door close and footsteps on the patio, and he was alone on the floor. The rapid voices on the TV built up a wall of sound that was too run-on to get, and he couldn't put a thought together, and for a moment he was terrified. He wanted to think a thought, but one wasn't extractable. The scorpion was small and translucent, the color of nicotine. He couldn't feel its weight, could only see it rise with his breath over his chest contour. Some of them would kill you and some of them were like wasp stings. He couldn't get the markings you were supposed to remember. The ones in Arizona killed you. He thought about Arizona. It didn't seem far away. There had once been a communication. Some were green, some were brown, he couldn't quite distinguish. Some were green and some were brown. You were not to be stung by the wrong one, but he couldn't remember which was wrong. His face was wet. The scorpion was rising and falling with his breath but hadn't moved of its own will. Quinn was bridged on the heel of his hand and could tip one way or the other by turning his head and breathing, but that might be enough to make it sting, and he didn't want it to sting. The TV was loud and the fat man still hadn't spun the wheel and the fat woman was all the way on her toes as if she wanted to fly and not come down until the wheel hit her number. He wanted to see the screen, couldn't keep his eyes off the emcee smiling and soaking up the situation, getting the studio audience involved. It seemed to involve him more than it involved the woman who might win something, more than anybody else. The scorpion suddenly seemed to wake up. It moved an inch on his chest then stopped, its tail uncurled. The Mexican suddenly dealt the wheel a huge, knee-bending haul, and the wheel chattered, becoming a whir like a mirage on the tiny aqua screen showing numbers and chances in a vortex, and then slowing as the balance on the heel of his hand gradually sagged to the side so that his chest tipped toward the TV and the scorpion slid off onto the tiles before the wheel had even completely stopped.

He bucked the floor and jerked off from the scorpion, which he couldn't see now, but knew would come after him once it hit the tiles. He slid on his stomach and kicked his knees so he could achieve a sit. The scorpion hadn't moved. It was almost invisible against the pale green tiles and gave no sign of intention. He pushed back to the wall and jigged his feet until the belt began to lariat around his ankles and he could get one foot free and force out the loop. The scorpion hadn't moved. The television was louder than before. The woman had caught her number. Peso signs were flashing on the screen, and the mustachioed man was talking as fast as he could and pointing at the woman accusingly, the woman was looking out through the peso signs in a fur coat, hugging herself and turning around and around in the commotion. Quinn advanced on the scorpion, his hands still wired. He came at it from the side, curling his foot, and slid it onto the space where he'd been lying, into the sweat circle on the floor. The scorpion sat on its stomach with its tail laid behind it inert. He suddenly brought his heel down and ground it on the tile. It made him mad for the scorpion to be still. The television was screaming and the woman was swaying in a daze, the coat hugged to her chest. The word *ganadora* had begun flashing below the woman's feet as if that was her name. It pissed him off. The scorpion had been dead, it was a nigger gimmick. It made you an asshole by making you be afraid of something

54

that turned out to be nothing. Though that wasn't precisely it. It was just all in behalf of what didn't matter. The thing that scared you was the thing that didn't matter.

He twisted his hands free, turned off the television, and picked up the Italian girl's underpants. His heart was hitting at the sides of his ribs, and his stomach felt turned over, beginning to cramp. Sonny was supposed to be the routine part of this. Rae was supposed to be the hard. Things were beginning to go off the track all of a sudden, and he didn't know exactly what it would take to get them on again. It was going to have to be Bernhardt's business, that was certain. Because his own progress meant to go in another direction.

7

THE ITALIAN GIRL'S perfume smelled in the bed. He had no
recollection from the night before, but it was all over the sheets
and on the pillows and the blankets. It had been on the underwear he had flushed in the toilet. A sweet, lemony smell with
sweat. It gave the filthy little bedroom a floating, locationless
feeling.

He took a drink of whisky and lay out on the bed in a nausea,
waiting for the pills to buckle onto the cramps. The cramps were
like animal pains, great slow fissures in his gut that were almost
too dramatic to be real pain, and you could suffer them out to
the point of amusement, the way a horse would when it got a
pain but couldn't recognize it for what a pain was, and liked it.

He had had his picture made two days ago in the park. He
could see it if he moved toward the bed table, himself in a white
sombrero and a red serape beside the posing pony. He wanted
to give it to Rae, but it seemed to fix time in a way he didn't
appreciate, put stress on his features he might not like in twenty
years, if whatever was happening turned out bad. There was a
picture taken nearly that long ago that showed him standing alone
on the sand beach on Mackinac Island, staring gloomily into the
camera as though into a dark thundercloud that threatened to

ruin his day. Rae said he looked saturnine and didn't like the pose. But the truth was that he had just fucked a big Finnish girl from Ludington, whom he'd met on the boat from St. Ignace, and who had wide Finnish blue eyes and dusty skin and was older than he was. And he was, he thought, in the best spirits of his life, and had gone back in fact, the very next moment, and found the girl and fucked her again. But in his mind, over time, he had defeated the facts, become convinced that he was sour and out of sorts, and he didn't like to look at the picture and kept it in his footlocker where he never saw it.

Time changed things, he thought, lying on the cool sheets with the Italian girl's cheap scent on him, and nothing more than the truth. He hoped in twenty years it would change the way he felt about this very moment, and that if he wasn't dead, he wanted to be able to think a good thought about it, and the picture, straining at the camera beside the pony, made him sure he wouldn't, as though the picture could trick you in some way you'd be sorry about. Being happy, he thought, and a pain flowered inside his gut, then subsided in a haywire spiral that the whisky controlled, being happy created problems, and not the least of them was being able to stand being happy.

8

IT HAD BEGUN raining in the Centro. Above floors, the air in the government palacio sat still and dense. Electric lights were off for siesta, and a sweet fodderish rain fragrance hung in the deputy's office. Outside it could've been refreshing, but inside made it oppressive.

Bernhardt looked uncomfortable. The set of his mouth was off some way, as if he had been asleep and couldn't quite get his features straight. It was a look that wouldn't sell tickets.

The deputy of penitentiaries sat behind a wide French desk. He wore a white silk camisola with expensive orange scrollery on the chest, and he was writing on a printed document that had carbons under it that required him to bear down hard. Each move was a precise move. Occasionally he would stop, turn, and look out the double window at the treetops and rain on the zócalo, then start writing again without speaking. The office had scalloped flutings on the cornices, and on the wall in the shadows was a large imperial portrait of Juárez in a red ermine cape and a gold filigreed crown he couldn't have lifted. The portrait had once been painted for someone else and Juárez's little rodent face added, so that he looked like a sideshow freak staring out from a body that was too large for him and that had him worried.

He was impatient to talk to Bernhardt. Deats was somebody you could handle, but Bernhardt had to do the handling. In the street big monsoon drops had begun smacking the cobblestones, and Bernhardt had looked preoccupied and hustled him into the palacio saying nothing except "It is important to be on time." But that wasn't enough. He wanted Deats seen to before Rae knew about him.

Bernhardt had on a clean suit, a white twill with European lapels that made him look larger than he was. His glasses shone in the deep shadows, and he was impatient.

The deputy suddenly quit writing. He looked up and smiled, lifted the document off the carbons and blew it. He rose slowly, carried the paper by its corner to the door, handed it to someone outside, then returned to his chair. "Momentito," he said amiably and pressed his lips together. He was a small, gold-toothed man and got smaller behind his desk. He put both his hands in front of him and smiled patiently so that the gold in his mouth leeched a tiny flicker of light from the room. "A seal," he said, nodding at Bernhardt.

Bernhardt had the money ready. Six fifties in a Holiday Inn envelope. He reached carefully toward the desk, not quite leaving his seat, put the envelope on the scrolled edge, and slid it forward to within the deputy's reach. "La petición," he said softly.

The deputy contemplated Quinn curiously and turned his head as though he heard a sound in the air that he liked, something in the rain hiss. He picked up the envelope, opened the belly drawer, and laid it inside. He looked back at Quinn with interest. "Is your friend?" the deputy said, folding his hands back on the desk top.

"Right," Quinn said. The deputy was an asshole, but that was a little luxury of taste he didn't own at the moment. You went through who you went through.

The deputy began shaking his head. "Is bad," he said and looked grave.

"What is?" Quinn said.

The deputy kept shaking his head. "Narco," he whispered and let his eyes go dreamy.

"But in a world of bad things," Bernhardt interrupted softly.

"Ahh," the deputy said and smiled. It was a sound he liked making. It pleased him into submission. Bernhardt had made the same sound in the morning. "Do you like Oaxaca?" the deputy said derisively, his spidery hands still composed on the desk top. It was beginning to rain harder, and the light passing through the trees behind the deputy had become an exhausted yellow blur. Quinn was ready to get out. He heard Bernhardt shift his feet nervously.

"Sure. It's great," he said finally.

"Es bonita, no?" the deputy said and smiled. "Is pretty, yes?"

"It's terrific," Quinn said.

"But it is not the United States, correct?" The deputy continued smiling as if they both could agree on that.

"It's got its moments," Quinn said. He glanced at Bernhardt.

"Maybe you would stay longer," the deputy said.

"I doubt that."

"Of course," the deputy said and nodded.

Steps approached the office door. A secretary, a Mexican girl in a tight skirt, brought the document directly to the desk. She placed it in front of the deputy without acknowledging anyone and left. A pen was in the deputy's hand moving quickly.

When he had finished he folded the document carefully, placed it in a fresh white envelope, and pushed it across toward Bernhardt. He smiled again. It was a postal clerk's smile, no special conviction. "Is dangerous," the deputy said, looking at Quinn.

"What's that?" Quinn said.

"Narco," he whispered, musing in the shadows.

"I wouldn't know about it," Quinn said. He didn't like the implication and he didn't like the deputy too much. Bernhardt was already at the door.

The deputy leaned backward in his big chair and opened his arms widely as if his appeal went out to a higher authority. "I know about it very much," he said and sighed, his chest heaving beneath his silk blouse. "It is a grave offense."

"I'll take your word," Quinn said.

"But I envy that," the deputy said loudly, letting his arms fall onto the sides of his chair. "You are lucky to know nothing. Maybe you will do well." He kept the smile frozen on his tiny clerk's face.

"I'm betting on it," Quinn said and followed Bernhardt out.

✳

In the courtyard a farmer in a straw hat stood beside a goat, sheltering below the arches of the palacio. A current of urine had drained from between the goat's legs out into the court and become diluted in the pool of speckled water where the center drain of the court was clogged. The farmer was looking straight into the sky as if he could see the end of the rain high up and was waiting for the moment when that end would arrive where he was standing.

"Deats showed up," Quinn said when they had stepped out to the cooler air of the mezzanine. It seemed believable to him now. Something about the deputy made it completely believable.

Bernhardt's mouth was nervous. "Where?" he said. He reached in his coat pocket for the envelope.

"At the bungalow." He watched Bernhardt closely for some sign of going down the road. "Something's got to happen right now," he said.

Bernhardt looked at him. "Do you want just to let it go? We can just let it go."

"That's not one of the options," Quinn said. "Think of something else."

Bernhardt stepped beside the granite balustrade that overlooked the court where the farmer waited, staring toward the sky. He put his fingers on the edge of the stone. "Does it matter to you if your brother-in-law did as Mr. Deats says he did, or that he didn't?" Bernhardt said. "A moral dimension."

"I'm not thinking about that right now. I'll think about it

later." He didn't like things that way, but they were that way. The moral dimension wasn't an issue.

"These are necessary questions," Bernhardt said.

"So what do you know about him?" Quinn said.

Bernhardt watched the farmer with the goat. "I know a man Mr. Deats has business with," he said softly.

"And?"

Bernhardt seemed to want to be very precise. "To deal with Mr. Deats in any way may damage their business, and then we are in their business. And that becomes risky. Do you understand?"

"No," Quinn said. "I just want to get Sonny out of the joint and the fuck out of here. Why is that risky?"

"I have to see the other people involved. I must impress Mr. Deats." Bernhardt was keeping his eyes on the courtyard while he talked. "That's the risk. It might be better to disengage."

"Are you talking more money?" Quinn said.

"No," Bernhardt said and suddenly looked at him significantly, though he couldn't be sure what the significance attached to.

"What happens to Deats?" he said.

"I will talk to him," Bernhardt said. He took off his glasses and held them up to the grey rain light that bathed the inside of the court.

"Is it easy?" Quinn said.

"No. It is not easy," Bernhardt said, blinking in the cool air.

"Is it dangerous?"

"Maybe it is," Bernhardt said.

"I don't want my wife in this." He tried to get Bernhardt's eye. "Do you understand that?"

"It is not necessary," he said. "She can go back. We do not need her."

"*We* need the money, though, right?"

"Of course."

"All right," Quinn said. "I just don't want her in any heavy-duty shit."

62

Bernhardt fitted his glasses carefully back over his ears and looked at Quinn calmly. "I will want you to come with me tonight," he said, "for business. I will explain to you." He began to walk toward the stone steps.

Quinn looked in the court for the farmer with the goat. They had moved back under the arches. Bernhardt appeared suddenly in the court below. He stopped and looked up and took his glasses off again in the shelter of the lower arcade. Quinn felt something changing imperceptibly, something that didn't make any difference. It was simply the less important thing you gave up, the slightest measure of control, he knew, that meant you wanted something very bad.

9

ON THE AIRPORT ROAD the rain was already past, dissipating
into the mountains above the bungalow, the airport obscured
out in dampness like a city eclipsed in a dream. The rented
Dodge had a radio and Quinn let himself ease into the jabber
of furniture sales and flights to Europe, good living south of the
border. There had been police in the streets when he had left
the palacio, too many for one afternoon. It had made the city
feel tense, as if the rain had left a film of dread behind it. Ugli-
ness went on at all hours, but you saw it by accident or not at
all. Something had made waves in the public sector, and Bernhardt had mentioned the shooting the night before. Everything
was ripples on ripples.

He had stopped at a tourist jeweler on the way and bought
a silver lavaliere with a green inlay of a man dancing. The sales-
woman was English and claimed the piece was jade and antigüedad and protective, but the inlay had been machined. It was
one lie or another, and for that instant all that mattered was
whether the woman had been convincing.

*

What had pushed it out of shape in L.A. had been the work.
He had thought if he could manage a union card somewhere

between San Diego and Santa Barbara and get on any place at scale, he could last a year, and something would get obvious in a year. They rented a house in the redneck suburbs back of Seal Beach a block from the navy station, and he had gone on weekends re-poing cars while he made the oil company offices all week and got his name on the master lists at Rockwell and McDonnell's and little feeder plants in Ventura.

Rae read magazines for a month, then went to work out of boredom ushering in a Jerry Lewis cinema. She started waitressing in a Redondo bar, then quit and spent a month answering the phone at a crisis center in Point Fermin until the crises started coming home, making her lose sleep. At the end she quit and stayed home watching quiz shows and reading *National Geographic*s stoned, until she decided the moral climate in California was oppressing. She told him she didn't like the weather being the same and the air changing colors, and that when she was with Frank Oliver they had gone north of Seattle two winters and stayed, and he worked the local rodeos, hung out, and moved cars into B.C., and she applied at the Swinomish reservation and taught prenatal care to give herself a life, and that she had liked that a lot better than L.A. She said she had read in the *L.A. Times* that people with factory skills were getting hired in Washington and the unions were opening up and she had an idea about Alaska. She said they could both work on the pipe and live in a house free and save twenty thousand dollars in six months and do whatever appealed to Quinn after that. She said she wanted to do whatever he wanted to do and stay together, and if he wanted to leave that was all right.

L.A. had begun to feel flatted out and unlocatable. He started hitting the fights on Thursdays when Rae was ushering, and going to the little social club arenas in the East End where the pure Mexicans fought, and sometimes to the Lakers with Rae when Sonny could get tickets. The fights had a discipline to them and a palpable life behind them, a coherence that was correct and apparent. Though he seemed to spend all day waiting for the night, and that seemed backward from how he wanted it. He didn't like re-po except it was the only weekend work, round the clock, where he could make enough to get by while he cruised Highway 1 with the phone book open, looking for job plants with a sign up for fitters, and waited up for calls. He began to spend every Friday afternoon on the bus to Lancaster or Mojave or Victorville, and every Friday night shadowing trailer courts and phone booths down the road from little four-room desert cracker boxes, wearing black jeans and a turtleneck, waiting for a sailor or a marine from Seal Beach to show up in his Firebird or his Formula Two and disappear inside. It was the wrong thing, but that was all there was he could stand. He could solve the routine and he needed the money. When the door closed, he would wait ten minutes watching, then walk to the car, check the back for kids or dogs, match the number off the windshield strip, slim-jimmy the door, cut the ignition, plug in the universal, and drive the car back across the desert to a big floodlit fenced compound in Downey where he could catch a ride to the Greyhound station on Main Street then start for another car.

On the last night he had walked up to a red Firebird—it had been a weekend of Firebirds—outside a one-row apartment motel in Oro Grande and slid inside without checking the back. When he started on the ignition a sailor with a chain dog leash grabbed him from the back seat and strangled him against the headrest until he lost consciousness. Two men drove him in handcuffs out to the desert between Yermo and Daggett, helped him out into the middle of the highway and started kicking him until he fell on his face, then kicked him in the ribs with tennis shoes until he went out again. The sailor had been waiting the whole time and the other one had been watching out the motel window. The last thing he remembered was the sailor asking, "What in the world do you want to do a thing like this for, man? It's a hard one. What do you want to rip us off for, man, we're Vets. Don't you know that? We're Vets." And they started kicking again.

He had lain on the warm asphalt watching the Firebird's red taillights being sucked up in the dark tunnel below the dazzle of L.A. sixty miles west, and he thought that the sailor had been on the money, and that if he'd been stupid enough to put in for it, the sailor had every reason to kick the shit out of him and leave him in the desert to freeze without any shoes. When he had gotten down off the plane from Guam, the very first thing he'd asked himself, standing on the tarmac at Pendleton, feeling lucky to be alive, was what had he won or how was he better. And at that moment he couldn't think of anything, though he figured an answer should've come to mind, a wrong answer at least, but not nothing—which was what he got. But in the middle of the night in the Mojave, he knew he'd at least won one thing, the right not ever to have to look up again and see taillights out in the cold channel darkness, the right not to be alone and busted up in no place he knew, with no place close to go.

When he got back it was Sunday morning, and Rae was asleep in the bedroom with the shades drawn. He sat on the edge of the bed and taped his ribs, turned on the radio, and made a call to Ronny Bliss in Michigan, somebody he'd known in high school and the service, and that he didn't care anything about, but who had told him once lying in the sun on China Beach that his old man worked for the state and could get him a job doing something at Natural Resources that wouldn't be hard to take and that would pay enough to live. It felt stupid at that moment to be going where he knew things instead of where you could find something you didn't know, as if unfamiliarity had a magic familiarity didn't. But his ribs hurt, blood was dry in his ear, and it seemed like the only thing that pulled the world together into an efficient place and had sense in it, and something that had clear sense was what he needed. It wasn't even the place as much as the sense the place made that mattered.

Late in the afternoon, Rae said Michigan wasn't a place she ever thought about going. She walked through the rooms in the house in her underwear and a purple T-shirt, smoking a joint, with sleep in her face. She said it was the wrong direction. She asked him why he didn't want to go to Seattle since it was closer and the weather was nicer and she could get a good job with the Swinomish or the Tulalips or anybody up the coast. He sat on the bed counting money. She had gotten him into this and he had made a commitment without knowing it, and she was something he thought he ought to try to do without. He hadn't told her about his Morgan money and didn't see any reason to. She hadn't said if she was going, and if the money wasn't in it, the break could just be clean. Otherwise he might find himself in a ditch some morning in the cold, without his shoes and his head singing the way it had this morning, and just figure the only thing for him to do was to crawl back out and go home and let *somebody* take care of him and tell him it's all right. In a while his ribs would quit hurting and his head stop singing, and he'd forget it. And that scared him. Wanting consolation was in you all the time, and you could get sucked up like those red lights in the night, and disappear altogether.

Rae was in the kitchen with the light on where he couldn't see her. He had $180 in cash and some checks.

"Don't you know progress runs the other way?" she said irritably. "You're just backing off."

"Let's just don't do that," he said. "I've been west enough." He wanted to get out of the basin by six o'clock. She could make up her mind by herself. She was just riding again anyway.

"What are you going to do if I *don't* go? she said. She had walked into the dark living room, her long hair around her face. He stuck the folded bills in his shirt pocket. He had his bags in the car already. "You just going to fuck whores like you like to?"

"And do dope," he said. He could hear her breathing.

"You wouldn't want to ride with Sonny down to T. J.?" she said.

"I'd rather re-po Plymouths and get my face kicked again," he said.

"I don't understand what's the matter with you," Rae said. She stood in the door. "You act like everything turned against you. You want to get rid of me? 'Cause I can just disappear, if you do. You know that?" Her eyes were wide. "I'll just disappear. You don't have to go to Michigan or wherever in the hell it is out there."

"You can go or stay," he said. "I thought you liked that. I'm sorry I don't have a big living room for you to ride in." The room was dark, but the light from the bed lamp made her features severe.

"I'm afraid I'll get off somewhere and *you'll* make a place to live, and I won't be able to, and it'll make me miserable," Rae said.

He walked in the kitchen, stood at the drainboard counting out cash on the rubber mat. "I'll give you a hundred and twenty," he said. "I need the rest of it."

She stood in the bedroom door. "You shithead," she said. "You don't care what I'm afraid of. You just care what you're afraid of, isn't that right? That's what conduct means, isn't it?" She wasn't crying yet.

"What do you want to do?" he said.

The dark behind her made her seem taller and frailer than she was. "Nothing's permanent, right?" she said.

"Nothing yet," he said. Light outside was the gun-metal color of first dark. He thought he could hear the ocean, but the ocean was too far away, though something always made him think he heard it.

"Do you love me?" she said. She had begun to cry. "You don't like to say it, do you?" she said. "It scares you. You don't want to need it."

"I can take care of me," he said.

"Then I don't want to marry you," she said angrily. "I don't want to be tied to you if everything turns to shit out there. You understand?"

"That's fine," he said. "But if you want to go, you better come on."

She left things in the house where they were.

✳

Ahead of him a Pepsi truck had driven off the airport road and blundered onto its side. All the Pepsi bottles had spilled on the ground and two Mexicans without shirts were standing in the field drinking Pepsis, other bottles already stuck in their pockets and down their pants. They were drinking fast, turning the bottles straight up in the air, though the truck was on fire and there was a chance it might explode. In the rearview he saw back toward town the red flasher on a police bus. Both Mexicans seemed to see the flasher at the same time and started running suddenly out into the muddy field that ended on the dry Atoyac riverbed. They ran like children, their arms thrown out wildly, disappearing abruptly into the chase of the river. He made a wide turnout to avoid the truck, a brand new cab-over Mercedes with PEPSI stenciled backward in red script across the blunt nose. When he got beyond the cab he could see in the mirror the driver inside, his face sprouting blood and jammed up into the windshield as if he had been trying to escape through the front of the truck when something came from behind full force and smacked him. Rae didn't need to see that. It would make her think the wrong thing, like the American girls gone out of the van in the morning. Everything got harder.

✳

The airport terminal was cheap tinted glass and concrete, and enclosed too little space. It gave you the feeling of having been half built, then abandoned, so that one end had needed to be blocked off.

Rae stood in the middle of the lobby, watching the soldiers. The other passengers had maneuvered themselves close to the baggage gate and were keeping their eyes on their business. The soldiers were holdovers from the interception, and were left around as cautions for new arrivals. They were combat-readies, and had done some shooting and looked serene.

"Does the army meet all the flights?" Rae said. The soldiers had begun leering at her.

"They think you're hot stuff," Quinn said, keeping his eye on the steel baggage doors. "Forty of them would be happy to show you a good time."

She took his arm and hugged it, ignoring him. She had on a green leotard, black jeans, and tinted glasses. She looked like a low-budget tourist. "Are you still protecting the deer, Harry?" She smiled at him.

"I gave it up," he said.

"You still let the marines cut your hair, though, don't you?" She intended to be friendly now.

"I wanted you to recognize me," he said.

"I'd always know you, Harry," she said and looked back at the soldiers, holding his arm tighter. "Big smile. Ecstasy on your face."

"Where've you got the money?" he said.

She pulled a strand of red hair away from her cheek. "In my Varig bag. I didn't think to tape it to my thighs."

A lot of money meant dope, and he wanted it brought in inconspicuous. No one checked luggage coming in. Coming in was easy. Getting out was the bitch.

He kept watching the gate. "My father died," Rae said matter-of-factly.

"Did he know about this?" Quinn said.

She had stared at the soldiers a long time. "He thought it was droll. He thought the maladroit ought to be punished." She looked up at him and smiled. "I'm a little stoned," she said, "but I'm glad you quit wardening. It didn't really suit you."

Soldiers could smell dope in a shit house, and no one could stop them if they decided to search you, like the college girls out on the highway. It wasn't smart. But she was freaked. "Are you holding?" he said, and took a look at the soldiers lining the exits.

She kept smiling. "I smoked a number on the plane," she said. "My last. I'm quitting in your honor. It just didn't seem right. Why don't you tell me how Sonny is?"

He didn't want to think about Sonny now. Sonny seemed a long way away. "He's alive," he said.

"What's that mean?"

"It means he's in el slammer. It's not a hotel."

"Is he getting out?" she asked calmly and looked at him. Her eyes were afraid.

"That's why I'm here," he said.

"I see," she said and looked away.

Taxi drivers had begun combing the passengers for fares back to town. "Downtown" was all they could say, and it was making the passengers nervous. Anxiety was your usual accompaniment. You flowed down it or you flowed against it, but you didn't float out of it. It was like the war, and you acclimated the same way, by never being out of it long enough to expect anything better. He felt like he'd made a good adjustment.

A jeep growled behind the accordion gate, and the steel doors suddenly banged up and the crowd moved in. Two fat Mexican boys began hurling bags through the opening. Across the plain of the Atoyac, the wrecked Pepsi truck was clearly visible in the distance. A long blanket of grey smoke had been persuaded back toward the city on the breeze that trailed the rain. Police flashers were swirling on the road.

"What's that?" Rae said curiously. She stepped forward and started out through the open gate toward the truck. She took his arm and kept him from moving up into the crowd for the Varig bag.

"I don't see anything," he said.

"Sure you do," she said and smiled. "That's exactly what you see. Nothing's innocent to you."

"I'm trying to lose that knack," he said. "It's in *your* honor."

She gripped his arm tighter. The soldiers were pointing out toward the smoke. "It's out of your control," she said, staring transfixed. "It's your instinct."

The other passengers were yelling in a confused English-Spanish and pushing bags back through the crowd. The taxi drivers had formed a line preventing anyone from getting to the exits. They stood holding white cards that said TAXI, and were smiling. The Pepsi truck exploded suddenly, a dark smoke puff followed by a bright orange swell. The noise took a second to arrive, and arrived diminished. "What's the matter with this place?" Rae said.

"It's full of Mexicans," he said, easing her into the crowd toward the gate. "Don't let it bother you."

"I don't like it," she said. "I'm sorry I made you bankroll this. I didn't know what else to do." She glanced at the soldiers uncertainly. "I don't know why I thought I had to do this."

"Because you love me," Quinn said, and put his arm around her.

"I guess that's it," she said. Her mouth was constricted. A short, fat Texas woman began giving her a deferential look. Rae pulled loose and let herself be pushed back through the pressing crowd, while Quinn moved toward the money.

✳

Where the Pepsi truck was burning there were a lot of police. Three blue minibuses blocked one lane with flashers popping, and several plainclothesmen with machine guns were marshaling cars onto the muddy shoulder. Stray officers were stopping vehicles and making drivers show papers. There was no reason for it, but there was nothing else for them to do. The driver was lying on his side on the pavement away from his truck, his face frozen and messed with blood. Some of the police were guarding him as if they thought he might be of some use later on. One of them was taking the driver's picture with a Polaroid. Quinn had his tourist card out, but when he passed by the policeman directing traffic, the policeman called "quickly, quickly," and waved him on.

"What's that about?" Rae said. She had the blue Varig bag on the seat under her arm. He had made her count the money in the parking lot, where he could see it. She turned and looked back at the Pepsi truck.

"An accident." He kept his eyes on the road.

"The man was dead there," she said. "His eyes were open." She didn't seem surprised. He glanced in the rearview. Some of the police had started drinking Pepsis. "All I've seen now are soldiers and police and dead people," Rae said. "Do you like it here?" She wasn't going to make an issue of the driver. It was a gift.

"It wasn't my first choice," he said.

She turned back and faced front. "Where'm I staying?"

"In the Centro. I've got you a room." It was a lie that didn't matter.

"Where are you?" she said, precisely.

He pointed up the Reforma Hill above the brown low profile of town. The white soffits of the bungalows shone above the palms of the nicer district nearer down the hill. Where the rain had cleaned the air, the bungalows seemed not far away. Behind them the rain glowered in the hills. A trace of the truck's smoke had begun stringing out into the green atmosphere. "Straight up," he said.

She took off her glasses, closed her eyes, then opened them widely at the mountains. "Is it pricey?"

"Nothing's pricey," he said.

"Then I'll stay there," she said.

"That might be weird," he said. He wanted her to stay as hard as he could imagine wanting, but he didn't want it taken for granted, and he didn't want her left there if Deats showed.

"Have you got company?" she said.

"Not just now."

"But you did have, though, right?" She looked over at him smiling.

"They think we're married," he said. "It makes better sense."

"Isn't that rich," she said. "Why would they care?"

"Maybe they don't," Quinn said. "Maybe I made it up."

"Fine," she said, and looked away. "Then I'll stay with you. I don't like to see failure in your face. I'm sure the Mexicans don't either. It's such an unusual expression."

10

WHEN HE WAS FIVE his father caught a sleeve accidentally in the belt mouth of a John Deere husker on a dairy farm outside Manistee, Michigan. And when the man who owned the farm, a Dutchman named Van't Hul, noticed him from a long way off, pulled flush against the husker's shiny green cowling waving his free arm in the air, he came running to see what was exciting. The hand was pulled in pieces when he got there to help, and most of it was stripped loose of the arm and the bones had jammed in the husker and shut down the works as truly as a piece of hickory. But when his father got out of the hospital, he set about to quit working farms and quit saving money for farmland and quit laying up surplus machines, and moved out of Manistee County altogether and into a rented stucco house with birch trees on Menominee Street in Traverse City and went to work for John Deere selling huskers with metal features across their conveyor mouths, using his new red stump for a selling aid. His father began to seem happier right away and laughed all the time and made jokes, and smoked big cigars and told his customers he enjoyed selling huskers more than he enjoyed working them, and that if he hadn't lost his hand to one he would never have gotten the chance to get smart. Though for years after the accident his mother would wake up in the night and scream "hand! hand!" as loud as she could because she had a phantom

dream where she saw it all happening again, even though she hadn't
seen it the first time. He could remember being nine and waking
up at night after the screaming had stopped, hearing his father
talking in the next room in a soft consoling voice, calming his
wife back into sleep. And when Quinn was thirteen, his father
told him, sitting in an ice hut in the middle of Traverse Bay, that
sometimes while he soothed her it was everything he could do
to keep himself from breaking out laughing, because he thought
that if he hadn't lost his hand and given up the idea of a farm,
he'd have gone crazy in no time at all, and his wife would've
left him as a failure, and his whole life and Quinn's too would've
been nothing but a misery from then on out.

※

In November, Quinn had begun running the deer tag stations
on the county roads between East Jordan and Mancelona, and
working nights in the D.N.R. Scout, sitting alert in the trees with
the door open to the frozen air, waiting to see a seal beam snap
on in the fire breaks or in the old white pine slashes, and hear
a poacher's .22 crack in the cold, and start idling toward where
the noise was, lights out. He liked that, the high-density sensa-
tion of solo work at night. It made you feel out of time and out
of real space and located closer to yourself, as if located was the
illusion, the thing he'd missed since he'd come back, the ultimate
good luck.

Rae hadn't liked things from the beginning. Quinn had bought
a mobile home in Traverse City and moved it up onto a finished
basement at the top of the bay where the birches and the alder
woods plugged the wind. She hadn't liked the trailer and hadn't
liked where it sat at the edge of a cutover orchard, too near the
timber for light to stay in the trailer all day. She didn't like
Michigan. She told him it was too glacial and ground down and
too bleak and uncharming to be a place where people lived. She
said she liked the West, liked the mountains, liked looking up
and down at things instead of across at them. She didn't like the

77

flathead bars and the no-menu cafés he took her to in Mancelona and Torch Lake and down in Traverse, wherever he was working. Sometimes in the bar light he'd see a face he knew, somebody from school, somebody he might talk to but didn't get around to talking to somehow, and it made Rae mad. And late at night they'd go home in the Scout and she'd be mad.

He began to come home mornings in the first December they were in the trailer and find Rae out of the bed, see her through the window, standing in her yellow parka at the farthest verge of the orchard where it swelled up into the alders, looking down at the trailer and at him when he drove up as if it was a sight that kept appearing to her in a dream, but that she couldn't believe really existed in her life and had to go out and stand in the clear cold and verify for herself every day. In a little while she would come inside where he was cooking eggs, standing at the stove in his undershirt and suspenders with all the lights on and the heat up in the kitchen and the grease thick in the air.

Once she said to him: "I never thought I'd live in a trailer in the woods with a game warden. You know that? It wasn't what I had in mind for myself when I was twelve."

He stooped and stared out the cold kitchen window at the fog running off the snow crust, swarming back through the bare white birch trunks into the denser timber. He liked the plain, compacted loneliness, the low almost pleasing pain of knowing nothing of any consequence was going bad for once. "I never thought I'd fly helicopters and pour shit on Chinamen either, but I did."

"You *wanted* that, though, didn't you?" she said.

"Sure." He watched the eggs casually where they broke up in the grease, turning pale.

"Do you have bad dreams about that now?"

"No, I never do." He thumbed down the heat and let the eggs rubber up and go hard.

"I just think, you know," she said calmly, and waited a moment. "I mean, I just kick around in here." She looked at him.

78

She still had on her yellow parka, her hair tied back. "I thought you'd ease up. I thought it was because of the war, but that's not right, is it?"

He slid the eggs onto his plate, carried the plate to the table, and set it down. "I could've told you that," he said.

"Why didn't you?" She smiled at him in wonderment.

"It didn't occur to me, I guess," he said.

"I don't know what you expect me to do," she said.

"Nothing," he said. "Anything." He began to eat his eggs.

"But can you please just tell me what it is you don't like or do like. I feel by myself even when you *are* here anymore."

He looked up at her across the table. "I don't know what I can do about that," he said. "You can be by yourself *with* me."

"And is that good enough for you?" she said.

"I guess so," he said.

"But what?"

"But nothing." He put his fork down and wiped his mouth.

"Is that all?" she said.

"I'm alone most of the time," he said.

She smiled at him. "Does that make you feel powerful? That's what the Indians think. They think it protects them. Except you don't need protecting, do you, Harry?"

"Everybody needs protecting," he said.

"From what?"

"From everything they don't know about."

"But why do you want to call that being in love?" she said.

"I don't know what else you call it."

She stood up from the table. "We make a hell of a couple," she said.

"Maybe I'm not a very nice person. You know?" He tried to catch her eye. "Maybe something ruined me."

"I don't know," Rae said. "I don't know what you are. But God knows I wouldn't want to violate you." She walked out of the room.

*

79

In the spring, Rae drove up to St. Ignace and came back with two registered Airedales she said she was going to breed because she'd always wanted a dog and now seemed like a good time. She hired a mason from town to lay a concrete slab twenty yards from the trailer. She had a chain-link fence built and a wood shelter put up and moved the dogs out of the basement where she had kept them and into the cage to wait for the female to come into heat while she read books about it.

In September, the female hadn't come in, and Rae began sleeping late and driving nights up to Petoskey taking any kind of J.C. classes she could get. In October, he caught his first two months working days, but Rae wouldn't come back from Petoskey sometimes until after two. The dogs would wake him up barking, and he could see the lights go on out in the enclosure, hear the gates clank, and hear her talking to the dogs in a sweet, coaxing voice. He would lie in the bed and sing a song, trying to stay awake until she came in, feeling like he missed her but that she was a long distance away, almost out of reach, so that when she came inside from the dogs he would always be asleep.

In late November, he went back working nights, and Rae began staying over in Petoskey, driving up on Tuesday and coming back Wednesday night, staying, she said, with a woman she met in her economic history class. They had stopped making love in the summer, after she got the dogs, and he had begun to feel as far back as then like he was running a skein out, but that he could stand it. He thought, sitting out in the frozen night in the Scout, drinking coffee and whisky out of a hot-flask and watching the empty ice huts speckling the bay in the winter moonlight, that the only dangerous lie to being in love was that it was permanent. And once you knew that, love didn't make you miserable, and you were safe from falling off too deep. In the best world it was a losing proposition, but even that could be satisfactory if you didn't insist on making up the loss, since you could erase yourself by mistake in the process. And he wanted to avoid that. He knew love's limits, and that was the key to everything.

On the sixth of December he drove into the yard before 5:00 A.M., when it was still dark in the orchard. The light was left on in the kitchen and in the dog cages, and the car was gone. In the kitchen there was a note taped to the window above the sink. It said: "Dear Warden, Just too dark in your woods. Love, R." He took the paper off the window and put it on the sink top and read it again. He had on his green state-issue parka with the silver badge, and shining out of the glassy darkness of the window, he thought he looked good enough and up to things, even though he felt just at that precise moment like a man falling, all out of attitude and disposition, from somewhere he didn't remember toward someplace he couldn't see. He walked back outside and across the frozen yard to the kennels. Both pens were empty and the spotlight over the gate was left on to warm the air. He looked inside the shelter but the dogs weren't there. The concrete had been scrubbed and ice had formed in the depressions, and the dog smell had gone thin in the cold. He walked back inside and went into every room in the trailer, turning on lights and opening closets. He turned on the radio in the kitchen to get the weather. He had the idea he should go in the basement and check the pipes and the water heater in case it snapped off cold. But when he got down the stairs where it was still and moist he turned on the bulb and looked at the water heater white and shining in the corner as if it were alive, and something seemed odd to him about it, something obstinate and repelling. He went back out to the Scout, opened down the gate, got the AR-16 out of the case, and went back to the basement and down the steps. He stopped at the bottom riser and chambered the first round, put his arm through the sling, flattened his back against the wall, found the water heater in the irons, and opened up on it like a range dummy, hitting it all over, blowing the fixtures off the top, blowing the brass medallion out and back inside the tank, and blowing the heater all the way off its base into the soft cement wall behind it. When he finished he turned off the light, put the gun back in the Scout, went inside, and ate some toast and stood watching the light grey up. When he'd washed the dish, he went back down and turned off the gas and the water in the basement, came back and took off his shirt, pulled out the phone, did sixty push-ups, and got in bed.

And he thought, lying there in his pants, what was his father's favorite thought, that every move was a necessary move, an emblem of something that needed to be fixed or set right in the everyday scheme of things, like a hand needing to come off, and what Rae had done was try to spark her luck the best she could by making a move. He didn't blame her for it, and even though it left him feeling for that moment like he was alone and falling someplace he couldn't see, like a dream in the dark, it didn't make him unhappy as an idea. The best thing you could do was to take events one at a time, in order, and hope one event by itself wouldn't cut you up too bad.

At eleven o'clock he woke up with the radio blasting Johnny Paycheck all over the trailer. He put on his parka, got the dead-dog crate out of the Scout, and brought it inside and shoveled the pieces of the water heater in it. He made coffee and stood in the living room with the door open, in the cold foggy light, listening to the furnace loading up and clicking, trying to keep the trailer warm, the flies buzzing at the windows, then took the crate out beyond the kennels into the snow and weed stubble and dumped it. Fog was expanding off the snow and clouding up into the alders at the top of the orchard. He took the box back to the Scout, shut the kennel gate, went inside and changed his uniform, and drove in to Eastport the way he dreamed he would when he had been asleep.

11

QUINN WANTED THE MONEY put away fast. Money gave him nerves. It was too important to fuck with. He got down on the bathroom floor and cut the grouting with his clasp knife. He took out six tiles and scooped a cavity in the dirt and laid in the four bundles of hundreds taped in sandwich bags. He raked the dirt back to level, packed it with his shoe heel, reset the tiles, and grouted them with Ipana he had bought in the Centro. He got up and turned the shower out onto the floor and let the water drain. He checked the tiles behind the toilet grail where he had the pistol. The paste there was moist and the tiles gave easily but not too easily that the moza would disturb them. The tiles were his own idea. He liked them.

Rae was sitting on the bed, her hands in her lap, the empty Varig bag on the floor. She looked confused and stoned. The room was dim and smelled like DDT. The moza had come and made the bed, but he hadn't noticed it until now. It was stupid to miss things. He was dropping habits.

"What have you got behind the toilet?" Rae said, without moving, her hands in her lap.

He wiped his hands on his pants. "Ordnance."

"Always a tough guy, right?"

"Eagle Scout. We always lead the survivors out," he said. He leaned on the doorjamb and squeezed dirt off his fingers. "It keeps me straight."

Light was failing except for a square, gold panel of sunshine on the floor in the living room. It made the bungalow appealing.

"You don't have any vices, do you, Harry?" She gazed at him as if she wasn't interested in the answer. "I thought you got cocaine from Colombia, not Mexico. Baranquilla. Isn't that right?"

"This is the peewee league," he said.

"What did they do to him?" she said.

He traced his finger down the rough door molding. "Nothing interesting. I think they tied a roach bag on his head. I'm not sure. He didn't know anything, he just *had* the right stuff."

"That's nice," she said.

"They try to be humane down here." It seemed like a waste of time to talk about Sonny. He stood in the doorway and admired her features relaxing in the green air.

"How do you feel?" she said, looking at him. "You look a little peaked."

He put his ear against the adobe. He could feel himself letting go a little. "A little detached. Like *I* was trying to bust out. I don't mind feeling that way usually. But I mind it now, I'm not sure why."

"Do you trust this guy Bernhardt?"

"If I knew him in the States I'd be sure." It was something the Italian girl had said the night before in the same bed, no reference frame. It was odd to hear himself say it. Someplace in the colonia a sound truck began to play a record of someone singing passionately about love. It was the everyday event. He couldn't understand the words, but the sound consoled.

"So who do we pay?" Rae said.

"A judge. But it's Bernhardt's trick."

"And what do I have to do?" She lay backward on the bed in the dying light and covered her eyes with her arm. His stomach flinched high up where a pill wouldn't help.

"Nothing," he said. "You can leave."

"Maybe I will," she said.

She turned her cheek against the bedspread and lay still a moment. "This bed smells like your last guest," she said.

He didn't answer. His mind wandered back up into the day toward the Italian girl but wouldn't reach all the way. Everything was the way he wanted it. She lay on the spread without moving, her arm over her eyes, talking into the air. "I discovered something, you know," she said slowly, as if she could see it out in the blindness.

"What's that?"

"Love is a kind of loss," she said. "You know what I mean?" She breathed in heavily. "I never realized that before I lived with you. You probably knew it, though, didn't you? Not that there's anything to do about it." The music truck wove through the terraces and down Reforma hill. She was waiting for him to answer. She knew what he knew. "You don't have any capacity for small talk anymore, Harry. I'm sorry." She leaned on her elbows and looked at him, her green eyes dry and blinking. "You used to, when we were in Morgan City. You used to jabber. And then you quit. I thought about that while I was gone." She let her head fall and swung her hair behind her. She made him feel kind. "Couldn't we make love?" she said, gazing at the ceiling as though she was talking to him there, somewhere up out of the cool air in the room. The music truck turned a corner and came closer, on a closer street. He felt transported now, somewhere indistinct, drawn outside of himself. "It'll change your luck." She put her hand out and touched his chest, measured his breathing, and smiled, and he felt bad luck moving out of him as if the atmosphere had become too fine for anything inessential to stay alive.

❉

At six o'clock Rae went into the bathroom and stayed a long time. Light was down and the mountains he could see from the bed through the window wore the same smeared patches of black, like silk draped beneath an orange blaze. It was the dangerous time now, the end of day, the time when prisoners in the prisión gave up and started patting their veins. It had become the worst time in Michigan when Rae was gone, desperation time, when the lake changed from the natural sequins of afternoon to dull oyster grey, and the first dim lights of the deep, white-fish trollers froze in through the gloom. It was, he thought, listening to the shower hiss behind the door, a bad time to be anywhere by yourself. It had come to be the time he liked in Mexico, as if the country was the tissue of everyone's loneliness.

He got up, put on his pants, and walked in his bare feet onto the little pink stone patio that opened on the city and the smooth white-rock roofs terraced into the evening. The air was damp and eucalyptus sweet, and he could see a long way up the hazy valley beyond where the city stretched to an end, to where the light was amber and smokes dwindled out through the palms from the pueblos you couldn't see in daylight. The city lay out in the dun darkness with no lights burning, as if the space were empty and there was no one alive for miles.

When Rae had been gone three months he had driven into South Bend and caught the train to Chicago to see a woman he'd met in a bar in Charlevoix, whose husband worked for a company that kept him in California. He could remember dozing in the parlor car in the early-morning silence, watching the snow fall in the Indiana freight yards, waiting for the train to move. While he sat, a string of cars was pulled away from near the window and he could abruptly see out in the yards toward the St. Joseph, where a snowman had been put up in the center of the eastbound main line to Detroit. The snowman had been built that morning. Its lineaments were crisp, and there were heavy prints flattening a circle around the base. The snowman was tricked out with gravel features, a blue and gold watch cap, and a half broomstick, and stood between the shining frozen rails, smiling perfectly into the face of its own hot doom.

When he hit Chicago it had stopped snowing and the wind had

settled, and the woman came uptown to meet him. He drove them in her car to the South Side into Hyde Park, where the buildings were old and elegant and built close to the street. At a stoplight a block from her house, a long purple Toronado with Indiana plates had eased away from the curb and blocked both southbound lanes, and Quinn had touched the horn to get past. But when he came abreast, the light changed red, and the driver of the Toronado jumped out of his car and ran toward him.

"Why the fuck did you honk at me?" the man screamed at him. He was tall and black and wearing a long leather jacket. He kept looking down the street quickly as if someone was watching him.

Quinn opened his window. "To get you off the dime," he said up at the man. He glanced back at the light.

The man's features began to strain, fighting a lawless urge inside himself, an urge that had an old-time hold on him. His mouth seemed to get longer, and Quinn recognized that look. It was the maniac expression of someone about to go to war, the look of fighting off cowardice with insanity. He sympathized, but there was nothing he could do. "You fuck." The man raged and stamped his feet and ground his hands together. But at that moment the light went green, and he looked up at the man and said, "Can't help, pal," and eased away, and the man suddenly swung widely, a hard plunging blow, that hit him on the arm above the elbow and tore a gash through his down jacket and into his triceps, spilling blood and down over the windowsill and making him barge into the other lane and jump the curb. The woman said, "Oh shit," and he began to feel the blood drying.

When he had bailed out, the man had run already to his Toronado and was racing up Kenwood Avenue, leaving Quinn standing in the snow in the middle of the street in terror, wishing he had a gun to blow somebody's head off.

The cut was superficial and didn't need stitches. The woman put Merthiolate on it in her bathroom and said she thought he'd been cut with a bottle opener or a key ward, and that the man had been swinging at his face when the car moved, and he had gotten lucky. His jacket was a loss and he had gotten blood on his whipcords, but when he had spent an hour with the woman in her apartment across from Jackson Park and the I.C., he made up a story that he wanted to see a friend who lived on the North Side, and took a cab up to Randolph Street and stayed all night by himself in the Holiday Inn overlooking the lake, unable to sleep until he could see the winter haze begin to brighten and clear toward Michigan.

But it had all given rise to a feeling he had never had before, even late in the war, down to days, a conspicuous undisciplined fear of enormous injury. A peacetime fear. Sitting out nights in the frozen basswoods below Elk Lake, listening for trolling motors easing down into the shallows of the Rapid River, sinking steelhead weirs between the first narrow sand shoals, he would suddenly sense something nearby, something that would hit him and blow him to pieces, and he'd pitch sideways in the Scout to miss whatever it was, though there was nothing. Delivery boys backing a TV out of an appliance-store door would make him scrounge up high in his stomach, ready to receive a killing blow. And at night in the trailer, barely asleep, there'd be the same galvanizing shock that threw him up in bed shuddering from the instinct that he'd almost been hit by something falling, though there was nothing to hit him, and no one in the trailer but him, and his pistol beside the bed. And every time he had the fear, he'd picture in his mind not the junkie who'd cut him on Kenwood Avenue, which he thought was the cause of it, but the snowman in the train yards in South Bend, standing erect and by himself, smiling out at some disaster rising up on the horizon.

He thought now, though, watching the lights beginning to prickle out across the valley and beyond the mountain rim like greying stars, that the threat of death in that instance was only the dark side of something else, something he needed—Rae, maybe—and would have to live with unexplained until he got it, or until he stopped wanting it anymore, and at the same time stopped wanting everything else too, which was just a disaster of a different order.

He began to smell the dense fragrance of other places, the evening coming slowly on the city, the pale nimbus of town light rising into the ash sky. Doves had settled into the eucalyptus branches, and he could hear a bus crawling up the Reforma Hill into the twilight. The music truck was gone and a sweet dirt and cinnamon odor shifted and wandered up through the evening atmosphere. It was the smell of town streets, emptied for the night except for the fruit stands and tortillerías out the Avenue Garcia Vigil.

Rae stood at the glass door, her hair thick and wet against her neck, her skin roughed and pink in the nearly gone light. He smelled her now, the sour streaminess of the bathroom and the sweet oil she used. She seemed taller than he remembered.

"Are we in the tropics now?" She pressed her hair between the folds of her towel, but he didn't watch her.

"The Torrid Zone," he said.

"It just feels out of date, to me." She let her head come to the side, letting her hair fall. "When I was in the shower I tried to think of one act of kindness between Sonny and me, you know, just something little. And I could only think of one."

He looked at her in the doorway, framed by the table lamp she had turned on behind her. Her breasts were full only to the sides of her rib cage, her head tilted against the doorjamb. Her body had a generosity that making love didn't have anything to do with.

"One might be a lot," he said.

Her face became composed. "One time, you know, when we were living in Bay Shore before my father decided to be an artist, Sonny was trying to hit a golf ball into South Bay, and I was standing too close behind him, and he turned around and said, 'Get out of the way, Rae.' And that was all. He thought he was a golfer. Isn't that pitiful?"

He could feel the air slide past his face into the open doorway. It reminded him of something from when he was a boy, something out of the lake after dark, but he couldn't think exactly what it was now. Something he'd liked, but lost. "You know what I'd like?" he said.

"Not to talk about Sonny," she said.

"That'd be all right," he said. "But I'd like it if you stayed a little longer than tomorrow."

She stepped across the flat stones close to him, the towel around her breasts. He smelled her skin in the air, felt the whorl of hair in the channel of her back. All the veins were blue under her skin. "Aren't you afraid?" she said.

"It doesn't matter," he said. He heard the clock strike seven in the zócalo and again elsewhere in town, seconds later. A dog began barking in the rich cabañas below the bungalow, a sound like a turkey's cluck, fast and frequent and disappointed.

"We make love at odd times, you know," she said softly, coming nearer. "Late in the day's such an odd time."

12

BERNHARDT WAS IMMERSED in driving the streets, as though he wanted to avoid something unpleasant. Quinn had left Rae in the Portal watching the Indian musicians preparing to play again in the kiosk. The Centro was crowded with evening tourists, and all the Christmas decorations had been turned on. He had ordered her a beer, and she said she could stand it an hour alone.

Bernhardt was still wearing the beige suit. He drove out toward the Avenue of the Niños of Chapultepec, which divided the middle-class from the poor districts, then switched back toward the airport highway. There were soldiers in the dark streets, patrolling specified houses, teenagers in camouflaged helmets sporting big M-16s. They looked condensed and undernourished in the shadow lights, like true guerrillas, their faces identical and obscure.

Bernhardt merged out onto the peripheral boulevard at the boundary of the slum barrios, into a district where the town buses turned back toward the Centro. There was little traffic, and the helium lamps gauzed the air and made it hang in the night. Bernhardt didn't speak. He drove a mile on the periférico, past the airport turnoff, then took a road that crossed the Atoyac and the train line from Mexico City, and went into the palms where there was suddenly no light, and the road became laterite. They were close to where the men beside the Pepsi truck had disappeared into the riverbed, and Bernhardt had begun to drive faster.

"Does it matter if you hit somebody?" Quinn said.

Bernhardt shook his head. He watched the road attentively as it narrowed into the dense palms. "The law makes more trouble than the good you do to stop. If no one is caught the death is bad fate. But when the law takes you, it wants to determine why things. *Why* do you do this? *Why* you do that? And if you don't mean to, there's no why, and they never let you go. But the man is still dead." Bernhardt elevated his chin in affection for his explanation.

"Where's this going?" He thought about Rae in the Centro. It was making him edgy to be away.

"It will take only a few minutes." Bernhardt flicked up the brights, and Quinn could see up the long corridor of palm trunks diminishing quickly into a hole of darkness. It felt like a picture from a dream in which events never completely conclude.

"Do you fear becoming old?" Bernhardt asked expansively, keeping his eyes on the road.

"I fear not becoming old a lot more," Quinn said.

"How many years are you?"

"Just thirty-one," Quinn said.

Bernhardt smiled. The dash light made the frames of his glasses shine. "For you, though, love is a place where you don't grow old. Is that right?"

"Sure thing. You put your finger right on it." He had a feeling he'd see Deats tonight, but he couldn't guess why. Bernhardt was trying to keep his mind occupied.

"I *do* fear it," Bernhardt said emphatically. He kept his chin high. "I am forty, a young man. But I consider sometimes suicide. It is only fear of being old, do you agree?"

"I go the other way," Quinn said. "At least I hope I do."

"You were in the war," Bernhardt said. "You don't think of suicide now."

"Maybe later," Quinn said. He stared at the undifferentiated wall of trees. "What's happened with Deats?" he said.

"Nothing," Bernhardt said.

"But it's getting done right?"

"Yes. But it is best to be very cautious now," Bernhardt said. "Mr. Deats is not a mystery. But he is a problem to be solved. And we must take pains."

Bernhardt stopped the Mercedes in the dark in front of what looked like an implement shed Quinn wouldn't have noticed in the trees, though the shed was built partway into the road so that you could hit it without looking for it, and past it the road quickly dwindled into a pony path and disappeared. The air swarmed up sweet and heavy in the darkness, and there was no noise besides the car ticking. Inside the shed a green candle struggled to illuminate a plank bar that had been set up on oil cans and a glass basin in the dirt underneath it with a hose siphon leaking some kind of mescal.

Bernhardt walked around the shed and into the gallery of bamboo, taking a blind path that led immediately past a row of rattan shanties with sheet metal roofs, lower than his head and invisible from the road. They walked into a shallow ditch and up beside what smelled like a trough of smoking vegetable refuse that made Quinn's eyes sting. Some of the shanties had papers on their fronts fanning a strike at the technological college, but no one was inside any of the doors, and the thought of a strike in the undergrowth seemed funny. The path through huts reminded him of two things at once, neither one funny and both dangerous: a *ville* on the coast below Phan Rang where there was a woman who had said something to him in French that he was willing to get killed to check out again. The other was of almost any place on any trail in-country that became a sudden killing zone, some dense place you took fire first at the waist, then the ankles, and had no place to return it, and lay shot-up, waiting until you got it stuck in your ear. Memory seemed like an account full of the wrong currency.

They walked until Bernhardt seemed to recognize one of the shanties and turned, his face pale and wide in the dark. He motioned with his hand and leaned through the mosquito netting that covered the door.

The air inside was cool and smelled like battery acid. Quinn felt exhilarated, though he was blind and his eyes were dilating too slowly.

Bernhardt suddenly struck a match and held it up. Against the straw wall was a wood cot and the outline of something white laid out on it. Above the cot was a poster of Elvis Presley wearing his yellow satin suit and red, white, and blue guitar, and looking ornery. When Bernhardt moved near the cot Quinn could make out a man in a muslin communion suit rolled up to the calves and a red sash tied in folds around his waist. The man appeared to be sleeping, though there was a long purple scar on his head that had cut off the helix of his ear, and made it clear the man wasn't sleeping.

Bernhardt knelt and put the match near the man's face. "Dionisio," he said loudly, as if he was trying to wake the man up. Bernhardt stared at the damaged face, which was candle-colored and had ulcers. "Hermano," Bernhardt said. Quinn felt suddenly that someone had entered the room. He turned and stepped back quickly, but no one was there, and Bernhardt's match died. He felt exhilarated again and unreachable, as though everything he had seen had been sucked out of existence. A second match hissed, and Bernhardt was looking at him, waiting for the light to make him able to speak.

"This is the man who sells your brother cocaine," Bernhardt whispered. The match plumed up brightly between his fingers. Bernhardt looked at the man on the cot beside him. "Dionisio," he whispered, and turned back toward the cot. He drew the match to the man's cheek, held it close as though examining something infinitesimal on the surface of the skin, then extinguished it there.

*

Bernhardt drove them back toward town quickly. The night felt appealing. Quinn wanted to let it go. Off the valley floor he smelled sweet Cordillera sage as they reached the vapor light and the empty boulevard where the city took up.

"What was the kid's name?" There was no reason to get worked up over a kid he wasn't acquainted with. Dead boys didn't bother him. But he didn't know why he had to see it. It made him feel set up.

"Dionisio Angel Perez," Bernhardt said casually.

"Who'd he run for?"

"Many," Bernhardt said.

"Deats?"

"Yes."

"So did Deats cut him?"

Bernhardt glanced at him sideways, then up and down the empty yellow boulevard as he crossed it toward the Centro. "The police catch him fucking with a woman in his car, you see. And they say he has to pay them money because it is illegal to fuck in the car when it is not for your wife." Bernhardt took a deep breath. "So. He give them money and they go away. But in a little while they come back, very borracho, and they say to give them more money. And Dionisio pleads he has no more. So the police go and bring machetes, they take him out into the trees and cut him. Then they run away to the mountains and we never see them again. Maybe they are guerrillas now." Bernhardt turned up the greasy cobbled street that ended in the lights of the Centro.

"Did you kill him?" Quinn said.

"No," Bernhardt said solemnly and shook his head, attending the street. They passed more houses guarded by soldiers who gazed at the car hypnotically. "The police," Bernhardt said. It was the story Bernhardt wanted to impress him with.

"Did *I* have him killed?" Quinn said.

"No."

"Did Deats?"

"The police," Bernhardt insisted and looked at him seriously. It was a warning.

The Mercedes pulled out into the Avenue Guerrero, which boundaried the zócalo. The Christmas lights were on in the trees, the kiosk was full of beige-uniformed musicians. The cafés were jammed, and the Portal was a carnival. He liked it that way at night, as if the day had condensed the best part of itself down to this. Rae was sitting where he'd left her, halfway down the Avenue Hidalgo side of the square, alone. Seeing her made him feel happy for a moment.

"Who else is involved?" Quinn said. He knew Bernhardt wouldn't wait and he wanted to know something important. Bernhardt wove through the wide street, eyes intent on pedestrians.

"You are," Bernhardt said casually. "But not in that way."

"Why do I have to be?" He glanced quickly at the crowds in the square, then back at Bernhardt.

Bernhardt turned down the south side of the zócalo and angled to the curb. "My father is dead, now, two years," he said distractedly, and paused a moment. "I have to leave my government career to come and support my mother and my brothers. I am like you in that way. I don't want to. But I am involved." He smiled, staring out through the windshield. "I leave *my* wife because it is too much in the country in Oaxaca to please her. She is a profesora." Bernhardt was staring at nothing.

"I don't know what the fuck you're talking about," Quinn said. "Does he get out now because the kid's dead?"

"No," Bernhardt said. He looked at Quinn now oddly.

"So why do I have to see that? Just for laughs?"

Bernhardt reached across and opened the door. "You will

96

know what I am trying to do for you now," he said. "You see what I have to see. You are involved."

The street noise blared inside the car. The band was playing exuberantly. Quinn got out and shut the door, then looked in through the closed window.

"Don't get me shot," he said through the glass. "I wouldn't like that."

Bernhardt shook his head and smiled, then looked at Rae. "In the morning we will go to the prison with your wife," he said. "Don't worry." He inched off into the traffic leaving Quinn alone on the street.

13

AT THE BUNGALOW he went straight to the money. The tiles were in place, and the grouting was firmed. It seemed too obvious a trick to pull, though he wasn't exactly sure, here, if he could recognize the obvious. But the tiles made him feel like he could trust Bernhardt, since if Bernhardt had wanted the money this would've been the easy way.

Rae sat on the davenport in the dark. He turned off the bathroom light and stood in the doorway where he could see out the window down the hill. The place he had been was straight off, beyond the Centro lights, below the distinguishable dark of Monte Albán. It was a place that didn't exist now.

"Did you think somebody was going to steal your money?" she said. She was calm, as though things were all happening to somebody else.

"There's that chance," he said.

"Are you worried?" Rae said. She shifted her weight on the davenport.

"Not yet," he said. There wasn't any reason to think anything but that Bernhardt was getting Sonny out of the joint. Sonny either got out or he didn't. Quinn wondered what Deats was doing, what was happening to him at that very moment.

"Is Bernhardt worried?" she said.

"He's not a worrier," Quinn said.

"It scares me," Rae said, though her voice sounded encouraged. "I don't want it to. I don't want to be scared. Isn't that ridiculous? I just got here." She got off the davenport and came and put her arms around him in the dark. "Do I look desperate?" she said.

He could feel her staring back into the darkness of the bedroom, her breathing shallow. "Not right now," he said.

"One of those boys in town asked me if I wanted to fuck him," she said sadly. "I told him no. But it made me feel lonely. Isn't that strange? I wasn't even mad at him. And then it made me feel scary." Her hair smelled sweet and thick.

"That's how you know you're grown up," Quinn said. "What used to make you mad makes you lonely. You find out you can't change anything." She wanted something, he knew, to make her feel better. "He was probably in love with you and couldn't find the right way to say it."

She put her cool hand on the back of his neck. "I don't like that," she said softly. "It's not funny." She was quiet a minute while she held him. It made him feel safe. "I didn't know if you'd come down here for me," she said. "I was afraid to call you. I'm sorry it's awful."

"It's gotten better." He put his arms around her. The measure of her ribs seemed almost too delicate and insubstantial to be actual.

"I'll tell you my secrets," she said, close to him. "Do you want to know? I've never told you."

"Some other time," he said. He put his fingers up in her hair where it was warm.

"Doesn't it bother you?" she said. His eyes wandered in the night sky. He didn't think he had a secret now. "I hate it," she said. "Nothing's worse than secrets to me."

He didn't want to think about that. He shut his eyes. His father used to say you didn't have to tell everyone everything, secrets were just ancient history. And he believed that. He thought there were a lot worse things to keep than secrets.

14

THE VISITATION SMELLED like it had been scrubbed with piss. It was prisoners' work, and the prisoners liked tricks. Half the ceiling lights had been turned off, and the cafeteria was cool and damp and crowded with American visitors, hippies whispering and smirking over the metal tables and the rest moms and dads in bright clothes, sitting erect, being cheerful and not noticing the smell while they chatted. It was the day for people without connections. Extra guards were at either end. Rae kept taking deep breaths.

They had waited an hour in an anteroom while Bernhardt entered the document of release and paid the alcaide two hundred dollars to keep his mouth shut until the judge could be paid. Rae had been searched, and when she came out of the room her mouth was closed tight, and she kept blinking as if the light was bright.

"My college degree isn't much good to me here, is it Harry?" she said to him, her hands tightly clasped on the metal table while they waited. She had brought two copies of the *Sporting News*. She kept her hands weighted on them.

"Try to smile," he said.

"Am I supposed to lead cheers?" she said. She had put on her tinted glasses and her hair looked darker in the bad light. No one was paying attention to them.

The *Sporting News* had a color picture of Hank Aaron holding a lot of bats. The values were all too harsh. It wasn't like life. "He'll be fucked up," Quinn said. "Just tell him not to do that. We don't want him hospitalized."

Sonny was let in the yellow door at the end of the room, searched, then released. His expression was different. It was as if he was thinner. Something wasn't quite right.

Rae began smiling when she saw him and kept smiling. When Sonny got close she reached across the table and tried to touch his hands, but he hid his hands in his pockets. "I'm fucking cut," he said and sat down.

"Oh Jesus," Rae said, leaning on the table still trying to touch him.

"Fucking shit, man." Sonny jerked his head angrily so his ponytail jerked.

"Just a second now," Quinn said. Sonny wasn't popped. His eyes were small and pencil-pointed. "Just wait a second." He was trying to put some ideas in front of Sonny to keep him calm. Rae looked as if someone had hit her face. She seemed to want to speak but couldn't. Quinn wanted her out, but there wasn't any way for it now. "How bad are you?" he said. He wanted to see a cut to be sure. This was something not to happen. He glanced at the picture of Hank Aaron with his arms surrounding the bats, smiling. It pronounced a malediction on everything.

"I'm all right," Sonny said in a soft voice. "I didn't go upstairs with it."

"Who did it?" He wished Bernhardt were there and Rae was gone. He could hear her breathing too hard.

"A fucking spic grease-ball. Cut me with a Sidra bottle," Sonny said, staring down. He was furious and terrified.

"Where?" Rae said. She had begun to sweat on her hairline.

"My thigh," Sonny said. He swallowed. He was scared but he wouldn't panic yet. He would panic later, but not now.

"Did you fuck with him?" Quinn said.

Sonny looked up fiercely. "I don't fuck with anybody in here,

101

man. I'm getting out, so I don't fuck with anybody." He looked at Rae as if he wanted something to hurt her feelings.

"It's filthy in here," she said and looked urgent.

Quinn still wasn't sure if he should believe it, but he didn't have any visible choice. "Can it keep?" he said.

"Maybe," Sonny said.

"Was it anybody you knew?"

Sonny shook his head. "Forastero," he said. "You know?" He looked at both of them blankly. He meant Deats.

"Just forget that now," Quinn said. "Just forget that." Sonny looked at him coldly with an expression of betrayal. It was an expression he had seen on Rae's face, but on Sonny it meant nothing to him. Americans at another table stood up and began embracing the skinny kid who had foot-fucked the Mexican girl. He still had on his "Try God" T-shirt, and his mother was crying and people were staring at her. Sonny glanced at her a moment and then looked back, uninterested. "Can you stay in one place?" Quinn said.

"Just *so* long. I gotta get the fuck out of here, you understand that. You don't hide in here."

"We got the document," he said quickly. "It's in the alcaide's office. A day now, all right? The money's here. Everything's here. You just have to stay still, you understand me?" The look of betrayal measured a state of shock, and that was all right if it didn't get worse. Sonny could suck it in if he wanted to. He just had to want to. "Kiss your brother," he said to Rae.

She looked surprised. "What?" she said.

"Kiss him, God damn it, let's go," he said, standing.

Rae put out her arms and tried to bury her face in Sonny's shoulder, leaning over the table awkwardly to do it. One of her tinted lenses fell out on the table, and Sonny let his arms hang. He hadn't said hello to Rae. It seemed like he wasn't sure what was happening.

"I'm sorry," Rae said. "Jesus, I'm so sorry."

"So fucking do something," Sonny said. He looked at Quinn

102

and smiled strangely, as though somebody had said something complimentary to him. "You're not in here, fucker," he said, and the smile disappeared. "I am. You know? I'm the one that's fucking in here."

"Just be cool," Quinn said. He touched Rae's arm. "Go now."

"We'll get you out of here, hon," Rae said.

Sonny gazed at her vaguely.

Quinn pushed across the two copies of the *Sporting News*. "Don't do anything stupid," he said, and led Rae down the row of tables.

∗

The sky outside was pale, as if a dead ocean lay hidden behind the mountains. Bernhardt stood beside the Mercedes in the gravel lot wearing a white cotton shirt in the breezy sunlight. "No troubles, correct," he said. He opened the car door to get in.

"Somebody stabbed him," Quinn said, when he got close.

Bernhardt stood up, squinting in the bright light. He looked as if he hadn't heard just right. "Who did?" he said.

"Deats," Quinn said. He looked at Rae, then came closer to Bernhardt. "This is getting real dicey, Carlos. You were supposed to see about this asshole, you know?" He didn't like having Rae hear this, but she was in it now, and there was nothing he could do.

"Is he all right?" Bernhardt said.

"He won't be very fucking all right long." Quinn lowered his voice. Some women vendors began to drift toward the car from around the prison gate. They had huaraches and pottery beads and stopped at a polite distance to hold up what they had. "I don't like the outlook," Quinn said. He looked at the vendors quickly. Rae was staring at them as if they had called her name. "I can get somebody else, but it's too late for that. You see that, don't you, Carlos?"

"Other people are involved now," Bernhardt said apologetically. "It has gotten complicated."

"Are you bailing out? Is that how complicated it is?"

103

"No," Bernhardt said gravely. His eyes snapped at the vendors, who were trying to strike up a conversation with Rae. They all said "trinkets" over and over and rattled their merchandise. "It will be settled tonight."

"That's what you said last night," Quinn said.

"You need patience," Bernhardt said and tried to smile.

"The man doesn't have time for patience," he said emphatically and pointed at the prison fence. "Somebody's cutting on him, see?"

Bernhardt's eyes flickered toward the prison. "At three today arrangements will be made."

"Not now?" Quinn said.

"It is not certain. But it *will* be."

"He didn't do it, you know that. He didn't skim anybody's shit." That seemed important to say. He wasn't sure why that mattered, but it seemed to.

"It's possible," Bernhardt said. He moved toward the car now.

"No. It's not possible." He took Bernhardt's bare arm. "He didn't *do* it, and I don't want him sliced like that kid you trotted out last night."

"I understand," Bernhardt said softly. "It will be done right."

"I need that, Carlos. I really fucking need that now."

Bernhardt looked away, out beyond Animas Trujano, where a circle of light illuminated the scorched valley floor as if somewhere someone was holding a magnifying glass to the sun. The light was almost pure white. He seemed embarrassed at being touched.

The vendors were smiling and holding out their Japanese crap as if they couldn't stand to have it near them another minute. "Let's just get out of here," Rae said. "They give me the bads."

"I'm not sure he understands it," Quinn said.

"He understands," Rae said. "You made it real clear."

Bernhardt began getting back in the car.

104

15

BERNHARDT TURNED WEST toward the airport instead of entering the Centro off the American Highway, and followed the periférico toward the east edge of the city where he had taken Quinn the night before. "I will show you a thing," he said selfassuredly.

The boulevard began to crowd with motorbikes and Zapotecs on foot as it approached the immediate plain of the Atoyac. There was a displeasing feel of rapid activity without a center to make it knowable, like a disaster area being evacuated. Where the periférico drifted north, returning to the American Highway, the foot traffic thickened and he saw out on the dry flats a wide unspecified expanse of earthworks like a garbage plain, only larger. There was a teeming of bodies in the empty expanse. Smokes were strung out vaguely against the noon light. The Indians on the boulevard were crossing and making out onto the flats with bundles of cardboard and car remnants held over their heads. People were digging and others were simply standing half-dressed among the heaps of dirt and cardboard, staring at the city as if it was something they wanted and were deciding how to get.

"Are those the people who eat garbage?" Rae said, staring interested into the sea of boxes and rubble.

"Marginales," Bernhardt said officiously, emphasizing the *g* in a way meant to impress. "Marginal people."

Bernhardt made a U-turn on the boulevard and stopped at the opposite curb. The camp had a wide public quality that made it seem knowable and unmemorable, like the faces in the buses waiting out on the highway. Humanity without secrets. An army jeep was moving slowly among the earthworks and cardboard hovels, its long antenna with a red pennant wagging listlessly in the sunshine. "They come one time, maybe for Cinco de Mayo, and then don't leave," Bernhardt said as if the sight was an understatement of a much more illuminating truth. He sniffed significantly. "I have clients here," he said. "They climb poles, take electricity, become a nuisance. Some are electrocuted. Sometimes the army comes with clubs and beats them at night. They have no rights, only needs, and so suddenly they are guerrillas."

"Am I supposed to sympathize?" Quinn said.

Bernhardt pulled the Mercedes down into gear and eased back into traffic. "It is possible to work here without sympathizing. Maybe I don't like your existence. But. . . ."

"What's that designed to do for me?" Quinn said.

"Your business is complicated," Bernhardt answered. "But it is not the only business. Everyone is marginal."

"Is that supposed to mean something?"

"The boy you see last night was a boy who lived there"—he motioned at the sea of hovels—"maybe a year ago, maybe less than a year."

"Maybe not at all," Quinn said. "Are you running for office, or working for me?"

Bernhardt wheeled the car back up into the narrow streets that led to the Centro. "You see in a tunnel. Outside what you see, things are not one way, but other ways at once. You need to be tolerant."

"It doesn't help me," Quinn said.

"Why don't you just shut up, Harry," Rae said wearily from the back seat. "Being an asshole isn't helping anything either."

He concentrated on the big Corona Cerveza sign he could see at night from the bungalow, blue-lit against the dark matter, a flat globe shining without motion, the continents shuffled to one side. At night he felt appealed to when he saw it, as if there were endless places to be, every one better than here, though he never believed it in the daylight, and didn't believe it now.

16

THE CENTRO FELT to him like Vietnam again, a crystallized stillness above the rooftops and a swarming, full-bore eeriness in the street.

Café tables in the Portal were jammed with tour-bus passengers drinking Cuba libres, and campesinos down out of the second-class camións milling in the sun, crowding the tabloid stalls. Bernhardt had left them in the middle of Las Casas Colón behind the Juárez Market, and Quinn had pulled Rae through the corridors of swaying meats out into the Avenue Ruyano between the banquettes of country flowers and Zapotec nostrums that cluttered the business end of the mercado. She hadn't mentioned Sonny. He understood she was storing that to deal with in private, and that that was the right way. She was giving him time to think of what to say.

He walked her up the busy perimeter of the zócalo opposite the Portal, toward the cathedral, and he realized suddenly he had no destination except to keep moving until three o'clock when he had to see Bernhardt. The zócalo felt weird. There were too many soldiers, as if the entire place knew something he didn't. He felt like they were on the run now. It was a new feeling, and he wasn't sure what moment it had come about, but it seemed for real.

"Where're we going?" Rae said and stopped in the street.

He looked around the Centro for a place to go. Nothing seemed very charming.

"The Victoria," he said. "You can have a sandwhich and watch the view."

Rae pulled a piece of her red hair nervously. The park photographers were mounting tourist children on white horses and taking their pictures while the buses waited. He remembered the lavaliere for the first time under the seat of the car. He wanted to give it to her, but the car was at the bungalow, and there wasn't time for it.

"Where're the whores?" Rae said. "That's all I know about Mexico. There're a lot of whores."

"Out in the soledad," he said. "You wouldn't like it."

"That's all I know to do, then," she said earnestly. "I don't want a sandwich." She paused a moment. "Who's Deats?"

"He's Sonny's pay master. He thinks Sonny stole what he was asked to pick up."

She stared into the zócalo. "Did he?"

"They think so. That's what seems to matter," Quinn said. He guessed this was as straightforward as it would get.

"Are they just trying to scare him?"

"We can't wait around to find that out. Carlos has to see about Deats," he said.

"I want to worry about that, but I'm losing it just a little now," she said. "I wish I was stoned. Wouldn't that be nice?"

They sat at the edge of the zócalo where the tourists wandered out of the park. It was market day and the band kiosk had soldiers in it, three boys with submachine guns, watching the promenades, while vendors in the basement stalls sold ices to the campesinos. A lot of blanket sellers were in the cafés and the sky had become waxy and hot. It made him feel as if bad things were catching up with him.

"Can you tell which ones are the French women?" Rae said and began fitting her lens back in her glasses frame. He watched two slender women walk arm in arm across Hidalgo Street and disappear into the arcade of the Portal. "They all have pretty ankles and little asses," Rae said speculatively, gazing at where the women had been. "They were on my plane yesterday. The blond one said that women whose chief asset was their looks only get praised in terms of age. They talked about that the whole time, in French, '*à les expressions de l'age.*' "

"Were they talking about you?" Quinn said.

"I imagine so," she said. "They're just cunts." She gazed up toward the government palacio. A contingent of police loitered beside the gate, M-2s slung over their shoulders. The army made the police nervous, and they stayed in the loggia, whispering. "Do you know why the Mexicans stare at us?" she said.

"They hate the fucking sight of us," Quinn said. She was doing it right, holding herself in, making conversation to make things all right. She never felt sorry for herself. It was admirable.

"That's not right," she said matter-of-factly. "It's because we have blue eyes." She snapped the lens into the frame neatly and began polishing it on her sleeve.

"You don't have blue eyes," he said.

"It doesn't matter," she said. "It's my discovery. I knew about whores, and I discovered that. I'm trying to be good." She looked at him prettily.

"It's because they can't believe anything they hate so much can look like you," he said to please her.

She sighed and leaned her face back into a rectangle of sunlight that had split through the jacarandas. "That's wrong, Harry," she said. "It's sweet. But you always make things seem worse than they are."

"Can you spot the narco agents?" he said, watching the stone plaza. There were more hometowners than usual now, big pale Midwesterners standing hoping to see something that would make them feel justified about leaving. They noticed all the wrong clues, and they made you feel abandoned. It was why he didn't like downtown at noon.

110

"No," Rae said, without raising her head to look, keeping her face toward the sun. "I don't look at things that way. I just see things as paintings."

A man was getting his shoes shined in the row of open chairs facing the taxi queue. He was a large handsome Mexican in a white camisa, with wavy hair and a bull head. He was lording over the boy below his knees, pointing to where the boy had missed a place. "Watches," Quinn said. "They coerce French tourists for their digitals. They can all say 'Give me your watch or I'll can you for drugs' in French."

"Did you ever do that?" Rae said. "Did you ever coerce anybody when you were a warden?" It didn't matter to her. It was just conversation.

He watched the agent step down off the chair and walk away without paying, the boy waiting in the sun, shielding his eyes. "Sometimes I'd hide south of Charlevoix and stop waitresses going south and make a deer check."

"Did that work?" she asked.

"About half the time," he said.

"Did you ever get a watch?"

"Never did," he said.

"That's too bad," she said. "Is that why you quit?" She raised her head an inch and looked at him. "Because you didn't get a watch?"

"I quit to come down here."

"Of course. Sweet man," she said and put her head back in the sun. "You're a sweet man, Harry. I thought this would be easy for you."

"It should've been," he said. "Nobody forced me to come. I'm a natural volunteer."

Across the plaza he saw a face he thought he knew, a face with a flat boxer's nose and wide, deep-setting eyes. The man was big-bellied with hairy forearms and wearing rubber-soled huaraches and a white T-shirt he'd sweated through. He was with a woman who was large and had on blue bermudas and a sleeveless blouse that showed fat arms. She looked shy and pale-skinned as though she might be getting sick. A teenage girl trailed behind them. She had on pink terrycloth short-shorts that bound in her crotch. The girl looked like she wanted to be doing something else. The man was pointing out fretwork along the mirador of the palacio de gobierno that he wanted them to look at specially. He was exuberant, but neither his wife nor his daughter was looking, and the man kept pointing, then looking back at them. The daughter was eyeing the soldiers in the band kiosk who were looking at her and smiling and whispering. The wife seemed not to want to think about anything, and her husband kept putting his hand on her arm.

He had thought for just a moment that the man was Frank Davito, a gunny from Minnesota who had had two wives at once. Davito used to say neither wife knew about the other one, though they lived two hundred miles apart, one in the desert near Hemet and one on the beach in National City, and each one loved him faithfully. Davito had said once, crouching in the rain and mist by the waffle iron at Khe Sahn waiting for chute drops off the C-130s, that he had figured out the happiest he ever was in his life was when he was locked up or in the war. He didn't have to think about the women then, he said. He loved to see them, but it never lasted long, and he couldn't stand worrying about them when he wasn't with them. It made him too empty, and being in the war gave him something else to think about.

"Take your business somewhere else," Quinn had said. The answer seemed obvious.

"Oh shit no," Davito had said loudly and smiled. "I wouldn't do that." He smiled even broader so Quinn could see his teeth behind a stubble of beard and mud. "I couldn't live without them."

"Then get rid of one," Quinn said. "Just pull her plug."

"That's too raw, Jack," Davito said, shaking his head. The draft off the big planes stung their faces. "That'd be like living in Minnesota again. I use one against the other. You can't fly solo." Davito laughed. "You need your little cushion," he said, and jumped out of the bunker and began running through the mud onto the open runway. Rounds were falling in, and Quinn squeezed deeper into the dirt, waiting for the next bird to bank out of the swirling clouds.

It made him think about the dead kid in his communion suit and half his ear whipped off. He seemed to have lost the cushion for it, the escape hatch to make that death not seem like his own death. And that was a cushion he needed if he was going to take this to the end.

The man who looked like Davito had strolled across the plaza and stopped in the sun at the edge of Hidalgo Street, hands in his pockets, looking longingly into the Portal, as if he wished he could get a table there where all the tables were full. The man looked like somebody you'd like, Quinn thought. His family was straggling behind looking inconvenienced. The girl in the pink shorts was still thinking about the soldiers and pulling her shorts down behind. The wife looked disappointed by how she felt and where she was. They seemed to be from Minnesota, and out of place on the zócalo in Oaxaca, and needed to be someplace where they could be happier. The man turned and looked at his family in a heartsick way, and when he did Quinn caught his eye for a long moment, as if there was something he wanted to say, though there wasn't. The man's family caught up with him at once and his wife began talking seriously, staring into his chest. His daughter had noticed Rae and was looking at her curiously, twitching her hip from side to side as if they were sharing something evil. The wife quit talking suddenly and extended her hands to prove they were empty and started walking away angrily, and the man looked back at Quinn and smiled and shook his head and stared down a moment, then stepped into Hidalgo Street to follow his wife. The girl waited a moment longer, entranced with Rae, until her father called and she turned away, her yellow hair catching a moment of pure sunlight.

The man made him feel like something was trying to get inside of him, something he didn't want, like a regret, but that regret was only the advance party for.

"I was wondering why the streets all changed names in the middle of town," Rae said cheerfully.

"Too many heroes," he said, "not enough streets."

"That must be a big problem in underdeveloped nations," she said. She put her arms around his shoulders and held him tightly. He felt the same thick ether of regret rising in him. "You can't let fellow Americans bother you," she said in a friendly way. "They're just in love, and they don't know how to express it. Isn't that what you believe?"

"Sure. Whatever."

"You liked those shorts too, didn't you?" Rae tilted her face back into the warm sunlight and closed her eyes. "Tight pussy," she said dreamily. "It's very stylish now in Moline or Carbondale, or wherever they're from. Maybe Charlevoix."

"I didn't last very long up there," he said.

She smiled into the sunlight. "You're a great kidder," she said. "You can't be serious a minute. It makes it all seem worthwhile."

"Just your bad luck," he said. "You might've hooked up with a comedian like your brother and had it all your way."

✳

The day had begun to hot up. Second-class buses wallowed in through the streets, windows full of mute Indian faces. Diesel had begun to overpower the sweet cinnamon smell filtering out of the mercado. All the fountains were on.

He watched the Americans emerge onto the Avenue Independencia from the Portal, and into the sun toward the Baskin-Robbins where the grate had just been pulled open and a boy was mopping in the unlit inside. The Americans stopped below a chiropractor's neon sign made to look like a spine, all the vertebrae curved and articulated, and bracketed to the chiropractor's windowsill above the Avenue Independencia. They stood beside the Baskin-Robbins, and the girl was staring up while her father pointed out the sign, sweeping his big arm up and down to explain the shape. His wife was gazing out across the street and imagining, Quinn thought, that the day was heading downhill. There was a brown dog standing beside her looking where she was looking. Her husband turned and spoke to her. Quinn could see consolation on the man's wide face. "I think knowing too much just makes you miserable," Rae said, for no reason, and at that moment the Baskin-Robbins exploded.

And for a moment you could see nothing, and then you could see everything.

There was one great bulb of orange flame roaring outward and bursting apart in the air, and then a huge hot noise, and then the air suddenly was emptied of sound and filled with a baked greenish dust. It seemed, for a moment, as if a meteor had hit the building. A bright green taxi that had been in front of the Baskin-Robbins was blown away from the curb and into the street, and the air seemed for a moment to be the color of the taxi reduced to dust. The Baskin-Robbins, Quinn could glimpse through the panes of rising dust, looked like a garbage can emptied and kicked on its side. Whatever was inside was blown outside now or gone altogether. The chiropractor's sign was missing. There were rag figures strewn on the sidewalk and in the street, but nothing was moving or flailing. Men began rushing off the adjoining street into the space of the explosion as though they were drawn in by the suck of air. Loud whistles were beginning. Tourists were running out of the zócalo in all directions. A woman screamed a long beseeching scream, and then a lot of people started yelling and the noise and swarming commotion took over.

Quinn was on his feet going toward the Americans or toward where they had been a moment before, but weren't now. Outside the park shade the sun was suddenly much hotter and brighter, and he could smell rank-burned metal and cordite. It was familiar and became almost pleasant when the air overheated.

A siren began somewhere out of the Centro, and he stopped

and looked at Rae, who was still at the bench, standing on it, her hands over her ears as though she could still hear an explosion. She had her glasses on and her face was unrevealing. He started back toward her through the mix-up of sprinting Mexicans chattering and searching all directions at once for a new peril. He was too used to being alone. His instincts were adjusted to that, but it was witless to leave her. Rae suddenly raised her hand and flung it forward, her face as calm as when she had turned it toward the sun. She thought there was no danger and he should do whatever he had begun to do. He stared at her a moment in the sunlight, then turned back to where the explosion had been.

Out in the street he saw the American girl's pink hot pants. They weren't on her now but were wadded into the muffling system of the taxi that had been blown over. He couldn't see the girl, though he saw her father, twenty meters down Independencia lying in a clutter with his white T-shirt blown off his shoulders and his skin blacked and starting to bleed. There was more screaming as more became visible in the street. The siren noise became more intense and nearer. Soldiers were coming from all directions, running with their M-16s ready at their shoulders, approaching heavy-footed and knee-bent as though they were receiving fire from somewhere, their mouths closed and drawn back, ready to shoot somebody.

He felt himself suddenly lose breath. His legs became awkward and painful, and he knew it was the way you felt just before you got shot, ultimate vulnerability. He thought about his gun, about the precise location of it in the bungalow, and the good it would do him to have it right now. None.

He knelt beside the American on the sidewalk and discovered his daughter was under him, odd-shaped and missing most of the part of her where her shorts had been. Her father was making a big blood bubble out of his mouth. They were both dead. He stood up and looked quickly for the wife, tried to find her white blouse in the rubble, but couldn't see her. The dog was sitting alone in the opening where the Baskin-Robbins had been. The woman could've been sheltered, he thought, but he didn't see how. Articles of clothing and peelings off the ice-cream machines were blown out into the street as though the explosion had curved as it went outward, throwing as much down-street as directly across toward the park. It made everything the same.

People were yelling in Spanish now very fast and loud, something he couldn't understand, that sounded like "I own her." He walked back into an area of sidewalk that was suddenly deserted, and he felt all at once that he was conspicuous and shouldn't be here and shouldn't let himself be separable at all. There was a theory for that too. Trucks were approaching. He could hear them straining gears. The sidewalk began vibrating. He posed an unreasonable risk now. On the front of the chiropractor's building was the long red and black boxing poster he had seen all week and that had not been touched. It showed two giant black boxers with their fists clenched in fight postures above the words "Sin Empate, Sin Indulto." No Holds Barred.

Soldiers had begun forcing people away from the Baskin-Robbins, pushing some unselectively, face-first into the wall of the chiropractor's building using their gun barrels, and kicking them in the hamstrings and yelling. The soldiers thought the bomber was on the scene and they were going to catch him, and Quinn knew if he didn't walk off the open sidewalk at that moment they would see him and take that occasion to arrest him. Firemen had begun covering the taxi with AFF foam, getting it on everything including the soldiers, who began kicking the people against the wall harder and pushing more people into line. The rag figures were covered, and he realized now he couldn't tell the woman from the mop boy if he found her. The commotion was maddening and all around, and he walked out into the Avenue Independencia and into the park through the crowd at the curb, away from where the soldiers were yelling and kicking people in the back.

Rae was alone on the bench, the zócalo having emptied. The

117

cab drivers and shine boys had all run out across Hidalgo, leaving their cabs and their chairs warming in the sun. They stood inside the shadows of the Portal with the tourists, whispering and gesturing toward the uproar. Rae sat facing the Baskin-Robbins, which was, except for two circus bubbles hung high on the building's façade, completely flocked in foam.

Quinn sat down without speaking and stared at the plaza. And for a moment, sitting in the sunlight beside Rae in the consoling wake of violence, he felt insulated from trouble, almost drowsy in the warmth of the afternoon. A monotony anyone could get inside of, anyone could feel safe in.

"Didn't you see me waving?" Rae said, her voice cheerful, though not looking at him. "I stood up on the bench and waved at you. I thought you saw me. You looked like you did."

"I saw you fine," he said. He let the drowsiness come down on him.

"Then you're just a stupid fuck, aren't you?" she said, her voice not steady now. She looked at him, her face wild. "It's the oldest trick they know. Set a bomb and three minutes later set another one, and you get the police and all the other stupid assholes." She shook her head. Her hair was damp. "You're fucked up. You're just fucked up. Didn't they teach you anything in the marines?"

"They lit that girl up," he said. Sirens were very near and more police whistles echoed through the empty park. There was a sudden, sharp pocking noise, close in, very fast, an M-16 going off at full, the familiar, unreverberating plastic noise, like a firecracker going off underwater. It wasn't a bothersome sound.

Rae stamped her foot on the pavement. "What happens to me?" She looked away from him fiercely. "You tell me, all right? What in the hell happens to me if you get blown up?"

He stared in the direction of the automatic weapons fire. It came from toward the Reforma. The soldiers had somebody trapped and were free-firing in on top of them. It began to be intense. "There's no way in hell those people could've expected that," he said.

118

Rae stared at him strangely. "What's the matter with you?" she said, unable to keep her head still.

"Not anything," he said. He felt tense now and his legs trembled. It wasn't a bad sign to tremble, it meant you were alert, and you needed to move. "I didn't see it right, that's all," he said.

A green and white ambulance truck turned onto the Avenue Hidalgo and idled along the perimeter of the park. The driver pointed to them for someone in the back of the truck, who suddenly peered out through the window. A two-way radio crackled inside, and the man in the window said something to the driver and the truck speeded up.

"Everything's gone so *bad*," Rae said. She was squeezing her hands in her lap. "I really can't do this."

"Yes you can," he said. "You certainly can. Let's get up." He heard more pocking sounds—thick, padded noises from streets much nearer. Something in the nearness alerted the soldiers in front of the Baskin-Robbins, and they began running toward the noise, their legs webbed with foam, their helmets and canteens bouncing, crouched in anticipation of shooting. The people against the wall began to stray away unhurriedly. It made him feel safe not to be interesting to soldiers or ambulance drivers. "Just stand up," he said. He stood and felt lightheaded.

"There's no place to go," Rae said helplessly.

"Yes there is, so just get up. It's fine." Water beat loudly in the fountains and the thop-thop of a helicopter somewhere too high in the haze to see began buffeting the ground. People in the Portal were staring at the sky.

"This is stupid," Rae said. "This is all very stupid." She was starting to cry.

"No it's not," he said. "It all makes perfect sense." He looked around the empty park. A green parrot stood out on the hot pavement perfectly still, its red target eye blinking at the sunlight. He took Rae's hand.

17

ALL THE COMMERCIAL STREETS up Cinco de Mayo had
emptied. No one cared to be on the street with soldiers, and the
siesta had begun. Every two minutes a blue minibus would swarm
by with its flasher spinning, and disappear into the Colonia La
Paz, where shooting was still going, leaving the streets back toward
the Centro silent and restricted. Whatever had made Quinn quease
up yesterday had begun to stroke again, and he was having to
down pills to keep his stomach from involuting. He didn't want
that trouble and he thought he could worry about the long-term
later.

He had found a driver and paid him to take Rae to Monte
Albán for an hour, then chauffeur her back to the bungalow via
the periférico. She had gone quietly into the cab, but when he
closed the door she rolled the window down and said: "Why
don't we just forget this now? I don't care anymore." Her hair
had come loose and her skin looked dry and pale.

"You should've figured that out before," he said.

"I'm sorry," she said. "I'm very sorry." The cab slipped away
and out of sight into the mercado.

He wanted the gun. The thought of the American with his

clothes burned off made him feel a way he hadn't felt in a long time, a way the dead boy out in the shanties and the American girl blown in two hadn't made him feel—that he could shoot somebody. Nobody wanted to shoot anybody until they saw someone they knew killed ridiculously. And then it became the only way to preserve importance and you couldn't back out. Shooting somebody raised your personal importance level, and that was necessary now. He knew he could work right up to it.

Bernhardt's office was on a hill block of blue and white flush façades with fake miradors above street level. The buildings were flat-roofed comerciales with steel shutters that opened directly to the sidewalk.

Beside the office door a carne carbón built out of half a five-gallon Pennzoil can sat smoking with strips of meat burning on the grate. A rooster stood beside the brazier and watched him approach. The rooster flapped its wings when he got close, as though it wanted to fly but had forgotten how. Quinn checked down the street for the tender. Two women were walking leisurely in his direction arm in arm, but too far away. The rooster had one leg tethered to a large rock against the wall, and after a moment stopped flapping and walked behind the brazier and stood looking up, noodling as if the silence had caused it to want to doze.

Bernhardt's office was a high-ceilinged room open to the street. A desk in the corner faced out and a few gloomy tube-steel-and-plastic clients' chairs backed against the wall barbershop style. The room was dim, though there was a zizzing fluorescent ring. Quinn disliked the office. It felt tired. Bernhardt told him no one trusted lawyers who were hopeful, and no one paid lawyers who were rich. Everything in the States was the opposite and better.

Bernhardt had his coat off, his silver pistol lay on the desk top in front of him. His hand wasn't far from it, but he didn't seem nervous. "Where is your wife?" he said.

Quinn looked around the room. "She gets upset when people

get blown up," he said. His eyes came to the gun. "Do you need that in here?"

Bernhardt smiled. He leaned his head a fraction toward the wall behind and opened his hands. "Ladrinos steal the paintings from the Palacio de Bellas Artes to hold for ransom." He made a wry face. "The bomb is diversion. But violence is promiscuous."

"What about Deats?" Quinn said.

"Arrangements are made now for Señor Deats." Bernhardt's eyes stayed fixed on him as if he was watching for a particular effect. "*You* are necessary now," he said.

"How's that?" Quinn said.

"To speak to someone," Bernhardt said, his eyes intent. Bernhardt picked up a silver letter opener from his glass desk top and held the point to the palm of his hand. The blade distorted the light back on his face. "Señor Deats has associates in Oaxaca who are unhappy with him," he said methodically. "Today I know this. They think he has treated them unfairly."

"Are they going to kill him?" Quinn said.

"No," Bernhardt said and shook his head slowly. "It will be painless."

"What happens?"

"It is my worry," Bernhardt said soothingly. "He creates his luck. Maybe it won't be bad."

"What are his friends mad at him for?"

"Business," Bernhardt said. "I am not involved." He closed his fist around the blade of the dagger and let his eyes fall toward it. "Don't worry about that."

Quinn thought about the Americans at the airport full of bullets. It wasn't how he had imagined things. And he had to let what he'd imagined slip away now. Bernhardt was lying, but he might not be lying about anything that mattered. It was just negative information, and he didn't have the luxury for that now. "I have to think about it," he said.

"Tonight." Bernhardt pointed the dagger toward the open street. "It must be tonight." A police van passed, flasher turning, but with no siren. Quinn could hear the engine strain up the hill.

122

"If there is martial law," Bernhardt said thoughtfully, "no one will come out of the prisión. So." He let his head roll back against the cushion of the chair and waited. The smell of burned meat hung in the office. It was a rotten smell and infected the air in the room. "What did you think you would have to do to get your brother out of the prisión?" Bernhardt said and pursed his lips. Bernhardt reminded him of the deputy of penitentiaries, a certain distance, a certain reservation now. He wondered what Bernhardt's was in behalf of.

"Who killed the boy?" he said.

"Who knows?" Bernhardt said placidly and shook his head.

"You work for them too?"

"I must know people who are not my clients." Bernhardt let the blade dance between his fingers while he thought a moment. His eyes half closed. "I am your lawyer. It is unreasonable to represent two sides."

Quinn stared at the silver Llama. It seemed sensible. He felt like he was being let inside something new that would be profoundly ordinary and profoundly predictable in every nuance, and that whatever was lethal in it would appear not to be, and vice versa, and for that reason was all the more lethal.

"What do I have to do?" he said.

Bernhardt leaned forward in his chair. Far out in the Colonia La Paz there was the chatter of small-arms fire and the wetted thop-thopping of a helicopter. It had become too far away to matter. "Tonight I will drive and get you. Your wife may come with us, it will not be unpleasant." Bernhardt had become businesslike now, as though he was satisfied by events. "Afterward. You will leave your house, I will have a hotel for you. When he is released, your brother-in-law will need to leave quickly. I have a turista card and a ticket. It will be smooth, but it is best to avoid the law still."

"What's wrong with the bungalow?" He was thinking about the money and about Rae alone there. It made his stomach tighten.

Bernhardt's features gathered gradually around his large mouth, which had become pinched in thought. "Nothing," he said. He looked innocently across the desk. "It is more efficient. You are leaving. It will be easier."

"Where's the room?"

"In the Centro," Bernhardt said. "The Monte Albán." His eyes shone.

"How safe is it?"

"*Very* safe," Bernhardt said confidently. He opened his desk drawer, took out a small photograph, and pushed it across the desk. A blond woman stood in what looked like a motel swimming pool, naked from the waist up. Her small breasts were nearly invisible in the baked colors and she was smiling hopefully, as if what was happening to her was not what she had expected but was something she was trying to get through.

"This is a woman I knew once in Texas," Bernhardt said confidentially. "She is not bad looking? Do you think?"

"No." Quinn put the picture back on the desk top. There was writing on the back side. The woman, he guessed, was trapped.

Bernhardt seemed pleased and took the picture back. "You should trust me now," he said, and smiled and put the picture in the drawer. "Maybe you don't trust me before."

"I trust you," Quinn said. "What's my choice?"

"But you should trust me as if you *had* a choice," Bernhardt said. "You have this against me now."

"I don't need anything against you." Quinn stood forward into the dim light. "That doesn't mean shit to me."

"It is an intimacy," Bernhardt said proudly. "As if we were friends."

"Any way you want it," Quinn said, and turned to leave.

Bernhardt smiled at him. "I invite you not to worry now," he said.

"That'd be nice," Quinn said. "But I don't think it's going to work out like that."

18

HE CAUGHT THE REFORMA BUS back up the hill. The bus
should have been empty in midafternoon, but it was crowded with
poor women and private-school girls in blue kilts riding home
to the wealthy neighborhoods, and beyond into the slum barrios
above San Andrés Huayapán. A soldier rode in the front step
well, but when the bus departed the Centro, he fell asleep against
his rifle and everyone became quiet. The schoolgirls sat stiffly
facing forward with their books on their bare knees, not looking
out.

The shooting in Colonia La Paz had stopped, and the streets
felt sealed off. The tortilleriás, the little cubed single-door buildings with names like Mimi and Fifi, were all closed and the
wooden doors bolted. A mist had burned off the hills and been
borne up, leaving the south end of the valley in a Levantine light
that turned the mountains gaudy, green and yellow and black as
far as you could see downrange. It was like a *National Geopraphic*,
a stricken landscape that appealed to you the moment you realized
you'd never be there. Only, he thought, he was there now, and it
made him feel on the edge of something dangerous, as though a
sense of lucklessness swam in the air around him.

His mother had told him once after his father had died that

the worst of the thirties in Michigan had been to see time making people luckless, people who had never thought of themselves that way, but who had had to begin thinking it because of money, becoming, as she said, a class apart and unreachable. When they had moved off the farm to Traverse City, across from them had been a big yellow house owned by some Jews from Grand Rapids, but in the late forties when his father was working for Deere, it had turned over and become a rooming house with a sign in front that said, simply, DIEL 33377. He couldn't forget the number now or the way someone had spelled *dial* wrong. After a while, the people in the neighborhood began to refer to it only as the Dial House and believed, with his mother, that the people who lived there were luckless, as though it was still the thirties and the people were pariahs. Cabs parked there long hours and sometimes overnight while their drivers were inside. Transients moved in and out of the upstairs in cherry time. New children turned up playing in the curb gutters summers, looking as if they had lived there all their lives. And his mother, with the other people in the neighborhood, disliked them, the tall knobby-faced men with long slick hair, and the children, dark and barefooted, and the tiny, silent Mexican-looking women you only saw in doorways. His mother pulled him inside when she thought he played with them or showed a tolerance for them, which he did. Some of them, he thought, were musicians, Southerners or men from Indiana, who played the local radio shows, and the women and children were their families. Though now, staring at the empty streets as the bus heaved across the American Highway and up into the better, upper-class neighborhoods below the bungalow, to wherever the rich schoolgirls lived behind walls, a long way from Traverse City, he believed they were just country people with nothing to live on, gone from wherever they had lived, ready to go anyplace to improve their luck. Maybe they would've done something illegal or violent, which is what his mother had thought and warned, but he doubted if there was ever any chance. His mother called them "common," which was a serious epithet in

126

Michigan, a notch above trash. And she said the word as if it had a bad smell on it, and didn't like saying it as much as she didn't like the people she meant it to describe. She thought, he knew, that his father's family, who were from Niles, had an impulse that carried them (and him too) toward the common, and that their tolerance for it was a weak board in the family character, weak and corruptible. And it terrified her the way moving off the farm had terrified her, the way the long grey expanse of the lake terrified her, the way the hand terrified her for what it meant. She saw it in his father and in him, and thought that she herself was totally incorruptible, and that she should encourage at least obstinancy in them both, which would do the work character and incorruptibility would've done if they had existed in them. It was why, Quinn thought, his father had been glad to lose his hand and quit farming and wanting to farm, and why his mother had waked up screaming. She didn't know when you'd gone too far with something and when obstinance and self-denying became a bigger threat than whatever loss it kept away in the first place. And his father, finally, had had to learn that in a hard way.

The point was, he knew now, after all those months alone in the trailer and in the Scout and out in the woods in the tent, that everybody lives in some relation to the luckless, whether they call it that or call it something else, or whether they manage to live near it or far away. And what mattered most was that you *knew* the relation moment to moment, like the one he felt now, the particular danger, so that your life turned out to be a matter of what you did to make that bearable, since you couldn't get so far away from it as to make it not exist. Though when you *tried* to protect yourself completely and never suffer a loss or a threat, you ended up with nothing. Or worse, you ended up being absorbed right into nothing, into the very luckless thing you were most afraid of.

He walked the last shaded blocks to the bungalow. Things were quiet and protected in the colonia, a universe apart from down the hill. Two of the schoolgirls got off and walked hurriedly the other way, talking in hushed voices. The Dodge was parked below the gate where he'd left it. He remembered the lavaliere under the seat, and decided it would go better when they were gone tomorrow. He wondered exactly how long it took news to get as far away as Minnesota. He thought it couldn't take long.

Rae was sitting in the living room beside the blank television. The light in the room was liquid and green. The floor had been scrubbed and a white film left on. He was thinking about the money. "Did the moza come?" he said, and walked to the bathroom. Grey water stood in a puddle at the base of the shower. He got on his knees and ran his finger along the groove. Water didn't matter, but the tiles could get stepped on.

Rae stood barefooted at the door watching him. She had on his plaid bathrobe. She looked woozy. "Do you think *she'd* steal it?" Rae said.

"Only if she found it," he said. He moved to the tiles behind the toilet.

"Do you fuck her too?" Rae said. "She's pretty. We exchanged nasties while she cleaned. She said you were very *amable* and very *generoso* with her."

"That's right." His knees were wet and the floor smelled piny where the girl had scrubbed with solvent and sprayed with O.K.O. She was a Mixtec girl with ulcers who was learning to read in the technological college. She had asked help with her letters, and he had demonstrated an upper-case *Q*.

He dug the paste with his fingers and lifted the tiles off the pistol. Water had seeped and beaded on the bluing. Grouting was already crumbled into the cylinder.

"Do you need that?" she said earnestly. She was holding onto the doorjamb, staring at the gun as if it were an odd color. She had taken something. But there was no use hassling it.

"You never can tell." He sat back on his knees and dropped the cylinder.

"Are you going to kill somebody?" she said.

He looked at her. He had just an afterimage of Deats' $200 alligator shoes standing in the filthy water. He was ready to shoot Deats now. There wasn't any more doubt. "Did anybody come?" he said.

"No," Rae said. She shook her head. Her face was pale in the aqueous light. He got off his knees and brought the gun to the living room where the light was truer.

"Did you like the tour?" he said. He sat on the davenport, tore a strip off his handkerchief, and emptied the rounds into the rest of it.

Rae sat facing him, her bare knees under the hem of the bathrobe like the Catholic girls on the bus. She kept watching him, holding herself together. "They have men up there who slip through the bushes behind the ruins to sell you jade. They whisper at you," she said. "I left when I saw that. It's all fake. They have them in Santa Fe at the pueblos. Some farmer always finds something. Antigüedad. It's just bullshit."

"The ruins are real, though, right?" he said.

"Do you want to know where I went when I left in the night last year? Or even why?"

He used the tine of his belt buckle to force the handkerchief down the barrel of the Smith & Wesson, then squeezed the nub end back through the breech. "I don't much care," he said. She seemed argumentative, and he understood it. He just didn't want to be that way now. The gun gave him a sense of relief.

She ran her hand through her hair and sat back in the chair. "I thought I'd try to find a place I liked, since I never had before. But I couldn't. Isn't that sad? It all seemed so bad. So I went to the dog races. I thought I might see where I went wrong. Just for luck." He picked up each cartridge separately and wiped it with the clean part of the handkerchief. They were still oily. He took the strip and pushed through each empty chamber. It needed solvent and the right brushes. Her conversation didn't interest him. "Then I went back to Tesuque, and then daddy got sick, and then I just sat around Bay Shore. I tend just to let things happen sometimes," she said. "I can't survive being alienated very long."

"You should've taken up with those high rollers in the plaid suits," he said.

"How did you feel?" she said, ignoring him.

He looked up at her. "You should've stayed around. You could've found out." He held the trigger and let the hammer ease in and out of the pin slot, listening for grit. There wasn't any, and he wiped the cylinder and began sliding the rounds back.

"I couldn't ever tell what the hell your life was in behalf of," she said.

"So do you know now?" he said.

"I forgive you, though," she said. He looked at her. "For being a fuck and for making me have to run out of there."

"I didn't want to have to ask you for anything else," he said. He put the last round in the chamber and closed the cylinder slowly with his thumb and his middle finger until the spring locked conclusively and the cylinder wound up to train on the pin. "I didn't want to get lost. Do you know what I mean?"

She shook her head. "That's not being in love."

"It's close though," he said. He took the gun and put it between the cushions of the davenport, not too deep to get at easily. He pulled it out and pushed it in. Deats would be in the bungalow again, and he wanted it set up right. The Italian girl's face rotated up in his mind, the thing about not having a clear frame of reference. He wanted a clear frame of reference with Rae, but it kept expanding all the time.

"Why does it just have to be close, goddamn it." She was crying, but she was Darvoned out, and she couldn't cry very hard. "I don't like that," she said. "Close isn't good enough. There's nothing nice in that."

He felt all right about the gun. He walked to the window and gazed over the terraced bungalows and TV antennas toward Monte Albán, south of which the sun was an orange helix subsiding into the mountains. "No, there's not," he said.

"It's just all a loss to you, isn't it?" she said. "And you have to prevent that at all costs. You have to keep yourself protected all the time."

"I think that's wrong," he said. He liked the dun texture of the mountains once the sun was gone, and the light was all residue.

"And that's why you came down here, isn't it? Because it's as mean as you are, and you can test yourself." She wiped at her eyes with her hand and glared at him. It was just leftover anger.

"I came because you asked me to," he said. "I thought there might not be another chance." He walked across the room.

"There wouldn't be," she said.

"Then I guess I was right," he said as he opened the door and walked toward the car to get the lavaliere. It was as good a time as there would ever be.

✳

After dark he lay on the bedspread, dressed, waiting for Bernhardt's car, waiting for the headlights to crawl the windows. He could hear insects in the wall behind his head. His stomach was quiet and emptied, and he felt articulated in the dark. He thought about a girl he'd fucked when Rae had left, a nursing-college girl from Ann Arbor, slumming in the ski bars at Shanty Creek and Mount Mancelona, east of Charlevoix. She was nineteen and had braided hair and long white arms, and seemed at ease being alone. When she had her clothes off, on the bed inside the trailer, looking cheerful as if everything was familiar, she said suddenly, "My father died last month, see, and I felt like no one had ever made an effort to know him, not even my mom." She smiled as if this was what she wanted to talk about more than anything. "And I was really tired, see, of hearing about movie stars and football players, all kinds of other people who had died." She stopped a moment and thought while she unpinned her hair. "A lot of great human beings die and never get any

131

attention, and it makes me angry. Do you know what I mean? They just disappear." She let her hair fall down and shook it and put the pins one at a time on the nightstand.

"I guess so," Quinn said, staring at his boots on the cold floor. Her life was complicated with events that obligated her, that were limitlessly signifying and engrossing, but that didn't make any difference to him. He tried to think of his old man and couldn't, tried to think if anybody had paid attention to his old man and couldn't remember. And it suddenly made him feel trapped, as if empty space was closing down around him, and made him sick with longing, a way he thought he wouldn't feel once Rae was out of it, but that he couldn't keep back now, a feeling of detachment and impairment, something he didn't want ever to happen and thought he had figured how to prevent, but had failed.

"I bet you were in Nam," the girl said and smiled at him happily and took his hand and held it to her cheek.

"What makes you think so?" he said.

"You got that tattoo," she said. "You don't look like a biker." She leaned to turn off the light. "But that's cool. You don't care about my father. We couldn't be here if you did, right? You'd have too much sympathy for me."

✳

Rae sat at the foot of the bed. He could smell her perfume in the dark air, could feel her nervousness. "I can't be ironic with you, Harry," she said quietly. "I sat out there and wanted to be but I couldn't. I don't protect myself well enough, do I? I just get mad."

"Do you still want me to protect you?" he said. He thought he might be able to, the first time ever.

"I don't know," she said. "I don't like the way you think about things. You look at everything like it disappears down a hole that nothing ever comes out of. And that scares me." He listened for Bernhardt's car in the street. "Doesn't that make you lonely?"

"That's not the right question," Quinn said.

"I'm sorry, then. What's a good question?" she said.

"Whether it makes any difference to me if I *am* lonely," he said.

"That's what scares me most," she said. "Because it doesn't, does it?"

"I'm trying to think it does," he said. She lay beside him on the bed, and he could feel her heart beating throughout the room. "I'm trying real hard right now to think it does."

"Then maybe that's a good sign," she said. "I shouldn't ask for a lot more."

19

MOST OF THE STREETS leading into the Centro had been barricaded. Garrison troops in orange helmets patrolled the coils of concertina wire separating the open streets, their small eyes glowering at the sweeping headlights. Something was on now. The town seemed safer, as if a lock of certainty had been put on public life. Bernhardt drove carefully. He took the narrow streets beyond the Juárez Market, and through the section where the overland trucks were repaired. Lights in the crowded bays were blue and phosphorescent, and men's legs hung off the open hoods. Acetylene smacked in the thick air and made the night appealing.

Bernhardt was weaving toward the carretera, staying near the curbs and making his turns elaborately. At an intersection the zócalo appeared suddenly back down the inky streets, the cathedral kliegs at the end gaseous and silver and imprecise. Soldiers stood in the middle ground, their rifles picketing the light, and the shrill sound of whistles came out of the dark. It was like Mardi gras, looking up Orleans toward Jackson Park at 4:00 A.M., the odd insulated feeling of time being lost.

"Where're we going?" Quinn said.

"The country," Bernhardt replied expansively. "Don't worry about the soldiers."

"What're they doing?" Rae said from the back seat.

"Searching for paintings, or what they can find. Terrorism is faulty, it exposes unexpected things. Other people's business sometimes."

"Like yours?" Quinn said.

"No," Bernhardt said and shook his head smiling. "My business is in the daylight only."

"I don't see why they close the main streets and leave the dark ones open," Rae said. Her voice was flat and expressionless, like the soldiers' eyes. She was staring at the dark buildings that slid by the edge of the headlights. She had on the lavaliere with the dancing man. The polished silver lit up the shadows.

"Some streets are secured so they may be used to different purposes," Bernhardt said, engaged. "In the dark if you are not the army maybe you are a criminal. And if there is a mistake it must be hidden." Bernhardt had on a shiny white camisola, embroidered like the one the deputy of penitentiaries had worn the day before, though more elegant and expensive. It made him seem more Mexican than before, as if he had shucked something self-conscious in his character that had never fit.

"What about us?" Rae said. "Are we mistakes?"

"No, no," Bernhardt said, watching the street. "We are different."

The car passed a street where troop trucks were stopped midway up the block, their headlights framing the wall of a building. Soldiers were moving in the light, but what was happening was unclear. Figures were passing too quickly. It was a police action. Quinn faced forward. You couldn't tell what was happening without getting up close.

"What happens if they blow up our hotel?" Rae said calmly.

"Don't think of that," Bernhardt said.

"I'm not afraid of it," she said. "It was just a thought."

"Guerrillas have bad timing," Bernhardt said apropos of nothing. "They are like children. Tomorrow will be safe. They forget." He smiled. More fast pocking sounds commenced someplace

135

nearby, and Quinn began to phase it gently out of the flow of thought.

Bernhardt took the highway north, the direction of no lights. Quinn let the air flood in, cool and without odor, no sage or the smell of corn being burned. It could've been anywhere, Michigan or Louisiana or California. No-place air. There were phantom cars on the road, coming high speed, Americans scared of stalling on the highway. Men with machetes wandering out of the agave fields to lie by the road. Everybody'd heard the stories.

The road edged the mountain terminus, then down again, and below toward the west was the migrant camp, unexpected, sprawled onto the tableland like a lake of subsurface lights, night smokes strung up feebly in the dark. It surprised Quinn the camp was here and not someplace else. In his mind it had been inside the mountains, and he wasn't sure it was the same camp as in the afternoon.

An inspection sat at the point the highway quit descending and flattened into the agave plats. Soldiers on the north side were standing under a lighted plywood shelter. They were drinking mescal from Coke bottles and moving into and out of the light with extreme deliberation. A corporal came to the window, and two soldiers pointed their rifles woozily at the car and frowned. Quinn tried but couldn't feel the danger, and smelled instead the thick boredom of the station. The soldiers were unnecessary to the frame of his intentions. It was part of the safety the town exuded. The soldiers were here to protect the citizens from the camp out in the fields. Bernhardt showed a card, spoke authoritatively to the soldier, then eased back into the darkness, and Quinn became soothed again by the night, protected and low, and ahead of him above the headlights the sky emerged night blue, encroaching by inches over the moon.

Bernhardt removed the Llama from under his shirt and put it under the dash. "People, guerrillas," he said distractedly, "sometimes they will shoot a car in town." He pulled gently on the pistol to test the ease of drawing it. "Now there is no danger." He glanced in the mirror at Rae.

136

"You want to tell us where we're going?" Quinn said.

"You must see Luis Zago," Bernhardt said.

"Is he your big shot?"

"Sí," Bernhardt said. He produced a Coke bottle of mescal from the floor. He unscrewed the top, took a drink, and offered it. The mescal had a nauseous citrus smell, a smell you couldn't drink, and Quinn handed it back. He wanted his stomach controlled, no panics. "He is an important man," Bernhardt continued. "He has no fixed ideas." He smiled.

"Like you?" Quinn said.

Bernhardt screwed the cap back on the bottle and set both hands on the steering wheel. He seemed to like the question. "Yes," he said. "But I am a lawyer, and even then it is not always convenient. Your business is not so convenient." He looked at Quinn purposefully as if he meant something he hadn't said.

Rae touched his neck softly. "Wouldn't it be nice to leave here at night," she said in a filmy whisper. "It'd be like putting things behind us, just losing them in the dark. That'd be wonderful."

"When we leave," Quinn said.

"Of course," she said. "When we leave. I meant that. I didn't mean tonight."

✳

What he could see of the house from the highway was like the running lights of a ship miles out, a giant hulk in the night moving at a distance impossible to gauge, on a horizon impossible to locate.

"Are we going there?" Quinn said. The sight impressed him into silence.

"Sí," Bernhardt said.

"My goodness," Rae said, her face up to the seat back, watching.

"It is la casa de Señor Zago," Bernhardt said. "And I only want to say," he continued patiently, "that if you have a pistol, now you should not have it."

"Why do you think I have one?" Quinn said. He tried to imagine how Bernhardt knew he had the gun.

137

"It will only cause you trouble," Bernhardt said over the steering wheel, watching the dirt road carefully. "We do not want trouble now."

He thought about the gun and the stupidity of not having it the moment he needed it, of the chance of seeing Deats and not having a gun then. The idea seemed funny, like the same stoned Ojibwas turning up again and again in the moonlight as if he'd come out but never been able to arrest them. He took the .38 out from between his skin and his belt band, put it in the glove box, and closed the plate. "Qué bueno," Bernhardt said and grinned. "It will be there when we return."

"What about me?" Quinn said. "Am I going to be here?"

"You too," Bernhardt said. "My word is on it."

Zago's house was a long, flat-roofed arrangement of stucco and glass cubes. With bright lights on inside, all the rooms visible from the road appeared empty. The most intense light came from a high middle casino with a cantilevered roof that opened to the sky and oversaw the valley south to the foot of the mountains. The night stranded the house against the inching clouds, and there was no way to tell what was around it or how it was distinguishable in daylight.

Bernhardt drove to the back of the villa where the approach became brick paved and opened into a floodlit court and garage. "Is muy elegant house," he said and smiled respectfully at Rae in the back seat.

"It looks like a convalescent home," Rae said, but Bernhardt wasn't listening.

What impressed Quinn outside was the absoluteness of the sky. It seemed to funnel light out of the courtyard and extinguish it like a blot over the rest of the world. There were no stars, and the moon had fallen below the roof of the villa and showed nothing. It made him feel precisely at the center of things, as though whatever was here had wicked the light out of the sky and focused it directly on him. Even with no gun, he felt competent and completely in control.

"Through the garage," Bernhardt said.

A door opened in the back of the garage, and Quinn went toward it. A mustachioed man in a white shirt and white shoes stepped half into the doorway, then stood back for him to enter. "Left inside," Bernhardt said softly from behind.

Inside the door was a narrow, half-lit corridor ending in another door thirty feet ahead. The air was oversweet, like a cheap men's room. It was an attractive smell, a smell you always thought you knew. The mustachioed man led them twenty feet down the corridor, then stopped and turned, pointing a long nickel-plated .45 at Quinn's mouth.

"No pistolas," Bernhardt said breathlessly. The air around Quinn's face felt suddenly congealed.

"Turn your back," the man said softly. He flicked the gun muzzle up.

It wasn't, Quinn thought, a threatening gesture. It was a businesslike gesture. The man didn't seem to care. Quinn turned and put his hands over his head. Rae stared at him, her chin up, as though she expected him to say something funny. The Mexican laid the pistol below his hairline and frisked his pockets, then moved the gun to the small of his back and patted to his socks.

"If you had a gun he would shoot you now," Bernhardt said from behind Rae.

Quinn could feel his heart slowing. He had the purest urge to lean on the gun, to come as close to it as he could.

The Mexican suddenly shoved the barrel hard against his spine. "La mujer," he said.

Rae's face changed oddly as if someone had stepped on her foot. She took off her glasses and pushed her hand back through her hair. "Why not?" she said and stepped past Quinn toward the Mexican and put her arms up.

The Mexican breathed audibly. He put the gun against Rae's neck and snaked his hand under her arms and down her front, over her breasts, her stomach, in her crotch and out quickly. Quinn watched for the little hand to linger, to choose a place it liked best, but it moved too fast and treated all the parts it touched the same, as if what it was after lay in an altogether different geography from Rae's.

The Mexican stepped to the side and pointed the gun at the door. "Ándale," he said.

"Just like high school," Rae said and turned toward the door.

The companionway opened directly into the high casino, which was large and elongated and sunk below the rest of the house, which led off into two softly lit corridors. The room had bright lights and a high cantilevered lucarne with opening machinery, and there were, Quinn noticed as he entered, long, heavy abstract paintings on all the walls. The paintings were bright acrylic and repeated one basic facial pattern in harsher and harsher distortions. The faces were female and ugly and static, like a design from another painter reproduced by a drugstore in sizes and colors to decorate anybody's home.

A small blond woman in a purple dress was lying on a sofa with a night mask over her eyes. She seemed to be sleeping. The Mexican brought them down into the bright room, and the woman awoke startled and pushed up the mask, squinting in the light.

She was American. Quinn had seen her in the Portal, drinking gaseosas with street boys. He had heard her speak in English, and there was something about her he didn't like. She was pretty and in her thirties and smiled too animatedly for the street boys, as if she liked thrilling them. Her features were small and delicate without makeup, and she seemed out of place with street boys.

"This is Señor Quinn," Bernhardt said politely, distracted momentarily by the Mexican, who disappeared into the far corridor.

The woman blinked in the bright lights. She stared at Rae as if Rae's presence in the room was something she didn't expect.

"They are Americans," Bernhardt said formally.

The blond woman reached for a cigarette in a glass bowl, and lit it. "What are you doing here?" she said. She examined the skirt of her purple dress, smoothed it, and blew smoke on it.

"It is business," Bernhardt said briskly, then addressed Rae. "Señora Zago is an artista." He gestured obligingly at the walls. "She is an expresionista. Correct?" he said.

Zago's wife stared at Bernhardt and took a drag off her cigarette. "Close enough," she said.

"Do you paint here?" Rae said. He knew Rae saw the woman had already singled her out, and was trying not to mind.

The woman slumped backward on the couch and held her cigarette out between her thin fingers. "The light's no good here." She looked disparagingly at her paintings. The face was her face. "Mexican light's too flat." She took another drag on her cigarette. "You don't look like you've been enjoying yourself too much in Mexico," she said.

"Señor Quinn has an amigo in the jail." Bernhardt made *jail* sound like *yell*. "Don Luis perhaps can help them."

"Why would he do that?" she said, staring at Rae again.

"Because he is generoso," Bernhardt said confidently. A door closed down the corridor, and the Mexican's rubber soles came squeaking on the tiles. Bernhardt glanced quickly at the entrance of the corridor. "He *is* generoso, no?" he said, looking back at Zago's wife.

"Very generoso," she said, and looked at Quinn for the first time. She seemed amused. "What did your friend do?" she said.

"That's not really the point anymore," Quinn said.

The woman smiled ironically. "Of course not," she said. "But you're ready to pay big for whatever the point is. Is that it?"

The Mexican in white shoes appeared at the head of the corridor and spoke something to Bernhardt. "Not that big," Quinn said. He looked at Bernhardt. He wanted to get to whatever they were here for.

"He must have something you want," Zago's wife said coolly.

"Nothing," Quinn said. "It's charity."

"Of course it is," Zago's wife said and leaned back into the cushion of the couch, still smiling. Her skirt had come halfway up her thighs.

"Perhaps you would wait with Señora Zago," Bernhardt whispered softly to Rae.

"But there's always a big price, isn't there, Carlos?" Zago's wife said. "I'll entertain your wife, Mr. Quinn." She blew smoke up toward the dark skylights. "We'll talk about you."

Rae glanced at Zago's wife, then uneasily at Quinn standing in the bright spots. She seemed anxious not to stay. "How long will this take?" she said.

"A moment, only," Bernhardt said encouragingly.

"We don't want to talk about you too long, Harry," Rae said.

"It will be no time, believe me," Bernhardt said. He looked at Zago's wife and touched Quinn's arm.

He walked between the Mexican and Bernhardt down the corridor toward a door half-open at the end. When they reached it the Mexican pushed gently into the room where the lights were off, and the green TV flicker made the air swim as if there was deep water inside. The room was tiny with no windows and no things on the walls. The air had the same sweetish men's room odor as the garage corridor had. Zago sat on a plastic folding chair by the TV, his elbows on his knees, watching a soccer game televised from high up in a stadium. Quinn felt the small muscles in his stomach coming taut. He had the feeling someone was going to hit him. The bodyguard shut the door and the sound of the Mexican announcer yelling into his microphone grew louder until Zago leaned slowly forward and switched off the sound. Zago had a kraut's face and dense yellow hair parted on the side like a schoolboy's. He was a thick, big man and wore a businessman's starched shirt and tie with suspenders that stretched his trousers up over his stomach. He was seventy and looked like a grocer. He had a kraut grocer's well-being and a kraut's fat body, but there was something in his slow formality that made Quinn certain he was Mexican.

"Do you like this game?" Zago said, still engaged by the screen.

"Not much," Quinn said. It made him uneasy to have Bernhardt behind him, and the air was too thick.

Zago looked up at him with an annoyed look. His eyes moved less quickly than his face. "Baseball?" he mumbled. "You appreciate *that* game?"

"Sure," Quinn said.

Zago set his hands on his knees. "Una pasatiempo, nada más," he said and shook his head. "It is not a sport," he said. He looked up at Bernhardt as if he was disappointed.

"That's if you don't like it. I *like* it," Quinn said.

"I *don't* like it," Zago said. His cheeks twitched. "Why do you want to have someone killed, señor?" he said.

Quinn glanced quickly at Bernhardt. Bernhardt was expressionless. "That's not what I want," he said. He looked at Zago again. "I want to get a guy out of the prisión. That's it."

"That demands that someone is killed," Zago pronounced solemnly, staring up at him without blinking.

"Not to me it doesn't," Quinn said.

Zago let his thick hand rise and fall back on his thigh in exasperation. "Your friend is a goddamned son of a bitch," he said. He caught a look at the flickering screen.

"I can't help that," Quinn said.

"He steals two kilos of Colombiano from me," Zago said, still engrossed by the set.

"He *says* he got something in a hotel room and the immigration police took it off him at the airport. He said he doesn't know how much was there." He felt uncomfortable standing in the room with the old man paying only broken attention. It was another waste of time.

"Why would you be here, Señor Quinn, if that was so?" Zago said patiently. He placed his hand on his chest. "He received four and two are not at the air terminal. I am not wrong."

"It's not what he says," Quinn said.

"And that is why you are here, Señor. Because what he says is not the truth. And you must help him."

"Maybe your kid only delivered two," Quinn said.

Zago looked at him and at Bernhardt, who had not uttered a

143

sound. "No," Zago said wearily and shook his head. "Not possible as a thought." He sighed. "Do you want to get your brother out of the prisión, Señor?"

"That's why I'm here," Quinn said. There was nothing else to say.

Zago tampered with a knob below the TV screen. The picture flopped sideways, then went right. "Then you must tell your brother to return the Colombiano, ahorita. Quickly." He nodded at his own words.

"What if you're wrong?" Quinn said.

"Then your brother will be in the prisión until someone kills him. And that will not be too long." Zago's fingers fidgeted on his legs. "Señor Bernhardt is a good lawyer. But he cannot make miracles."

"What about Deats?" he said. He was trying to locate Bernhardt in the transaction now, figure just when in the scheme Bernhardt had come to seem like a good idea to Zago.

"Mr. Deats has difficulties," Zago said softly. "He can go on with his difficulties or we can stop them tonight. Depende."

Zago was going to kill Deats no matter what, he could just take his time or hurry. That was all it came to. Whether Zago hurried or didn't hurry. It was simple.

"And what if I don't convince him?" Quinn said.

"I think he will be reasonable," Zago said. "He will speak honestly to you. *I* have convinced him." Zago stood. He wasn't as big as the impression he gave sitting down, he was only slow and heavy-boned. "When I am young," he said expansively, "I am myself a socialista, like you, like my wife." He smiled as if the thought both pleased him and amused him. He put both his hands under his suspenders. "It is in my heart. But I found out it is necessary to work to live. My son is now at Stanford." Bernhardt was opening the door behind them. He had not spoken. Zago extended his thick hand. "Happy dreams, Señor." He smiled. "Y buena suerte."

Something had been decided, and he wanted it clear. "What about Deats?" he said.

"Do not worry about Señor Deats," Zago said consolingly. "He is no longer your problem. He is mine, now. And I will protect you." He held out his hand and Quinn put his in Zago's large warm palm. Nothing felt under his control. All his choices were made for him. Sonny had the only option that mattered anymore, and that was exactly, he figured, the way God intended it.

20

RAE STOOD BESIDE the Mercedes, waiting for Bernhardt. Quinn stood in the middle of the court, watching the garage door. There was a chill now that the floodlights couldn't warm, but he didn't want to get in the car yet. He was working through Sonny in his mind, figuring just exactly what the responsibilities were, at what point you had to bolt. Sonny was stringing it all out and he was having to put it back right. And that made him feel stupid and mad.

"Zago's wife fucks Bernhardt," Rae said calmly, tapping her fingers on the hood of the car.

"Is that it?" he said.

"It's like he wants to believe she won't surprise him anymore," she said. "Except it worries him. It's real queer. Maybe it's just Mexicans."

"Did you like the paintings?" he said. There was no use talking about it. If Bernhardt wanted to put that up as earnest money he could. Somebody always fucked somebody else, but nobody gave a shit.

Rae thought about the paintings for a moment. "They were just therapy," she said without an edge. "She wanted to know if I loved you. She asked me if I thought love was visible and uncontingent. Isn't that sweet?"

"What was your opinion?"

Rae turned toward the open end of the court where nothing was visible in the darkness. The question seemed to have an extra dimension. "I told her it was. I didn't really take to her." Rae seemed isolated in the court, almost unreachable. "What was Zago like?" she said.

"A grocer," he said. "A fat old grocer."

"His wife's much younger," she said.

The door opened and the Mexican in white shoes leaned out, holding the knob. Bernhardt emerged after him, and Quinn began walking toward the car.

"Sonny's such an asshole," Rae said. She was looking at where the stars should've been.

"We're way past that now," Quinn said.

"But I want you to know I know it," she said and took his arm. "My motives weren't very pure; you're aware of that, aren't you?"

"I've always suspected it," he said. He opened the back door to let her in the car.

✳

The lights at the army inspection had been turned out. Soldiers still lingered in the shadows, drinking mescal and gazing into the dark. Low lights glittered across the fields where the marginales had settled. Their effect was of great inertia, of no life, like a photo negative held to a dim light.

Bernhardt took a drink from his bottle and gave it over. The air in the car was cool. Rae had gone to sleep on the back seat.

"What is it like to wait?" Bernhardt said. He seemed at ease and drove with his elbow out the window.

"It's boring," Quinn said, "mucho boring." The mescal made a warm place in his gut. It was smart to use it now. It would make him sleep without pills. Mescal was the pure distillate of drunkenness, and that's what he wanted. It was worth risking bad dreams.

"Fastidioso," Bernhardt corrected and smiled. "In Spanish, means to be too careful. Maybe you are too careful, see too narrowly." Bernhardt looked out at the black highway. He was cheerful. "Your wife is beautiful, you have nice memories together, your senses are engaged, you should take pleasure in what's pleasurable, not be bored."

"Is that what you do?"

"If I can," Bernhardt said agreeably. "It is a way to take perspective on good and evil."

"O.K., so what's evil?" Quinn said.

Bernhardt looked at him as if he should know the answer. "Feeling so bad," he said and smiled.

"And what's so good?"

"Not feeling so bad," Bernhardt said, smiling more broadly. "I don't think that's the way you see it." Bernhardt looked at him as though it was a joke.

"Was it tough finding me?" Quinn said.

The car neared the first confluence of city streets. Vapor lights drifted up the periférico, but there was no traffic. The empty boulevard opened wide and gaseous into the distance. The city was sealed. Bernhardt took his pistol from under the dash and put it inside his shirt. "You found me, I think," he said. "No?"

"I want to know what your part is in all this, all right?" Quinn said. He wanted, for once, to see all the lines run back to origin. It was just a matter of seeing it done. That was all you could get out of it now.

"I am like you," Bernhardt said briskly. He fingered the frame of his glasses so that they sat higher on his nose. "In by accidence."

"You're not Zago's man?"

"I work for you," Bernhardt said confidently. "You find that impossible?"

"You didn't know Sonny was asshole deep in with Zago? I'm supposed to conclude that?" He had hoped Bernhardt wouldn't run it back this way.

"You pay me for what I know, Mr. Quinn," Bernhardt said. "It's possible to know a thing, suspect a thing, but not to be compromised." He looked across the car amiably.

"Why make me see that boy, then?" Quinn said.

"For me," Bernhardt said quietly. "I told you. You are in Vietnam, but this is a different thing. You need to *see* what you are involved in here. It's better." Bernhardt's eyes were bright and glimmering. He took another strong drink of mescal. "You say you like to see things. You should trust me," he said and smiled.

"Why did Zago zap him?" Quinn said.

"Señor Deats," Bernhardt said authoritatively.

"Then how did you even know about it?"

"Someone says to me, there is a boy who is injured in the cabañas, I should be interested. It is a gesture. Señor Deats and Señor Zago have difficulties. I don't know about them very much."

"So what's the mechanism?" Quinn said.

"Señor Zago trusts you," Bernhardt said. "Your wife's brother will be released, put to an airplane, and you will return to Señor Zago what he asks for. No holdups."

"I trade myself, then," Quinn said.

Bernhardt seemed sympathetic. "*Sí*. But. Then you will be asked to trust your amigo and not the dueño. He understands that. That is better too."

"And what if I don't?"

"Then you should leave the country now," Bernhardt said. "I wouldn't blame you. You owe nothing to me."

It seemed like the point he'd been working down to the whole time, the point of taking Sonny's place, some necessary penance.

"Do you recognize the woman?" Bernhardt said. He seemed pleased with himself.

"I don't know what you're talking about," Quinn said.

Bernhardt looked at the periférico without interest. "In the mansión. The woman there?"

"I didn't recognize anybody," Quinn said.

"Bueno," Bernhardt said, and turned off the periférico up into the dark streets toward the Centro. They passed the calle de putas. Rae was sleeping still. Bernhardt glanced sideways, but the street was empty, and there were no lights burning along the little block of whores' cribs. "But you do see what I risk for you, though. You see that? It's as if we are friends."

"Sure," Quinn said. "That's great."

"That's all that matters to me," Bernhardt said. "That's enough. Tell me what you dream about, Señor Quinn."

"Getting out of here," Quinn said. "I don't have room for anything else."

21

TWO WOMEN SAT in the Portal de Flores, drinking beers and talking in the blue fluorescence. They looked like English women. Something in the way they sat in their chairs, too straight, holding their beers with their fingers extended. The Centro was empty except for a few police and the soldiers in campaign coats shadowing the street corners. As they passed it, Quinn peered in through the pink, Moorish arches of the Monte Albán, where they would be in an hour. He thought, for some reason, he might see Deats there. Lights inside were blue and filmy, and he could see into the atrium, the skeletal dining tables set in lines. Nobody moved and there was nothing else to see.

"I need to telephone," Bernhardt said in a businesslike way. "Then I drive to get your luggage."

Bernhardt didn't notice the soldiers. He turned past the university buildings up Cinco de Mayo and rolled noisily up the cobbles.

The streetlights here were pale and gauzy. A dim, prestorm clarity froze the façades and made the sky flat and seamless. There were no cars on the street and no one was walking. When the Mercedes stopped, the street was silent and Quinn listened for sounds in either direction and heard nothing until the air softly began a low sibilance that covered everything, like the night expiring.

"Momentito," Bernhardt said. He smiled at Rae on the seat, and got out. He unlatched the steel shutters on his office, pushed up the door, and walked inside, switching on the lights.

The rooster and the carne carbón were gone. A scrim of papers was wadded against the façade, with the rock that had kept the rooster in its place used to hold the papers down. He watched Bernhardt at his desk, dialing the phone, looking silently out at the car. He could remember catching a frog in the saw grass along the Boardman River and bringing it home while his mother slept and letting it sit a long time in a pan of water on the back porch of the first house his father rented when they left the farm. He let the frog stay in the pan until late afternoon, when the frog had accustomed itself to the house air and grown calm. And when the frog stopped paddling and began to sit still for minutes at a time, he carried the pan in the house and down the hall to the kitchen and set it on the gas and lit the ring at the lowest flutter of flame and stood beside the stove and waited. The water in the pan began to heat at once, though the flame was low and the change was gradual. The frog sat in the water and looked up at him calmly and didn't move. And little by little, he turned the knob and watched the flame fatten and turn bluer and the frog sit in the warming water looking out, blinking and breathing, though never moving, until suddenly a fizz sparked the edge of the water, and he saw that the frog would sit and stare out past the time when it could move even if it needed to, and he took the pan off the flame and held it under the kitchen tap and watched the frog blink and blink, its mouth opening a little and closing, beginning to paddle about until it could escape if the danger was from drowning and not from boiling. He thought later the frog in the pan was an illustration of how people let certain things they're used to go on so long that they don't know that the things they're used to are killing them. And he wondered now, sitting in Bernhardt's car, just when that point exactly was, and how you knew when it was close to you, and in the rare event you did know or could guess right, just what you did to keep yourself from getting burned.

A campesino turned the corner two blocks up Cinco de Mayo and started slowly down the hill toward the Centro. He was a small man in duck pants and a straw hat woven to give the brim a deep-swept country flange. He watched the man, noticed the way his feet moved near the ground, his gait regular and effortless as if he was accustomed to walking long distances. The man reminded him of the farmer with the goat in the palacio court the day before.

In the office Bernhardt had begun speaking into the telephone, watching the open door, his eyes moving. He picked up the letter opener and held it by the blade while he talked. There was no way to guess at the call, or its importance. It could be something else, and Quinn looked back at the campesino, who had crossed the Avenue Absalo and stopped under a lamp, gazing back up Cinco de Mayo as if he was searching for an address he had lost. The campesino had a rough beard, but his shoulders were loose and his head was erect and he was young. He stood in the streetlight ten meters ahead of the Mercedes, peering disconsolately back up into the darkness of the avenue, and Quinn could hear again, then, the low sibilance in the street, the soft ventral suspiration of any city, Chicago in the blue morning. Detroit deserted at the moment the sun set. It was the sound of sleep, and it put you at ease.

The campesino started suddenly toward the Centro, his sandals slapping the pavement quickly, though as he came in front of Bernhardt's office his head turned as if he'd been surprised by the light, and his hands seemed to move excitedly under his poncho. There was a sudden loud expectoration of noise then, and the campesino was wrenched forward barging into the open door. The view to the office became lost then, but the light licked out either side of the man, printing him in the doorway as if he had stepped behind a shade. Quinn yelled into the whacking of the machine gun, but the campesino seemed to get smaller and kept the gun pointed in the office the entire time. There was a fountain of metal shot away from the man's body, and then suddenly it stopped. And for a moment, almost a leisurely moment,

153

there was no movement and no sounds anywhere, and it was as though what had happened, something he hadn't even seen or been sure of, hadn't happened, and everything remained the way it had been just a moment before.

Rae was crawling across the back seat on her knees, trying to reach the floor. He grabbed her head, losing his breath, and caught her front and back and squeezed until he could feel movement go back in a shudder down her spine. He put his face in her face and shook his head *no*. Rae's eyes were large and expanding, her hair was falling around his hands, but she understood and went limp.

When he looked back the campesino was up Cinco de Mayo running toward the streetlight. He turned the corner onto the Avenue Absalo, where he had stopped a minute ago in the light, and disappeared. On the pavement there was half a gun of some kind with a long clip out the side and no stock, something Quinn imagined at that moment would be very hard to fire well. It had a length of cord tied to the barrel and the trigger guard, and it was rocking back and forth on the clip butt. There was a heavy odor of eggs fried too long on dry metal. And the time seemed to pass in a kind of dreamy slowness. Bernhardt was still inside the office, though the light there seemed much brighter and the air in the street too warm. Bernhardt had moved from where he had been. He was against the back wall and to the right, nearly out of the door frame. His pistol was lying in the middle of the floor in front of the clients' chairs. His shirt was torn across the front and he was bleeding onto his arms. His face seemed unperturbed, but he was lying in a strange leg-over-hip position that Quinn recognized, and that no one who was alive would try to maintain. Bernhardt's hand was tapping the tile floor spastically, but that movement didn't mean anything.

He had squeezed Rae's face until it was cold and there was a heavy faintness on her he could smell and that suddenly seemed suffocating. He shoved her up and toward the car door and said, "Out, get out," and began struggling to get himself into the street.

Time seemed to speed up then, and he felt the need for cover. He thought he had at the most a minute, and then there would be no more chances.

Rae's lips were pressed tightly against her teeth, and she seemed heavy and in danger of falling down. She hadn't spoken, and he turned her toward Absalo in the direction the campesino had run, and where there were no sounds in the street and no motion up the flat façades. He couldn't make himself think of Bernhardt, though he thought a lot would come to him later and that everything was changed beyond retrieval. Below them, the Centro lay in a smear of lights and trees, and beyond that above the buildings he could see the blue Corona Cerveza globe shining on the still night. Anyone who saw them now, he thought, would know where they came from, and it would be over.

"Don't run," he said. He reached back in the car, got his pistol, held Rae under the arm and shoved her. He took a last look at Bernhardt. He was small on the office floor. His glasses were on his face, but his shoes were off him as if he'd been blown completely out of them. The telephone was replaced in the cradle, and the wall behind where he had stood was unmarked. The campesino had hit him with every round he fired and only stopped when there wasn't enough left to shoot at. It was skilled work, something Bernhardt wouldn't have expected.

Far up Cinco de Mayo there were headlights. They startled him because they were coming against the traffic, and at a speed only the police would come.

They reached the corner of Absalo, and Rae continued walking out into the intersection. Her eyes were fixed and wide and she made an attempt to pull him.

"Just do what I tell you," he said, and jerked her backward. She looked at him, her eyes beginning to move a little, but her mouth still against her teeth. He thought for an instant she was going to speak, but then saw that she couldn't and that it was not speaking that kept her on her feet. He looked back at Bernhardt's office—the Mercedes, the doorway bleeding light, the gun alone on the pavement, and the casings still rolling down the gutter—and he was almost for an instant overcome with a giddy thought-erasing fear that he was going to die and it would be the wrong time for it.

The Avenue Absalo was dark, though there were regular stanchions lighting each corner block after block. The street was a comercial with pink and pale blue adobe façades. A sweet bakery smell floated in the street, and Quinn scanned the storefronts but nothing was unfamiliar and there were no alleys or cars parked, and no one was visible down the street except a man at the first corner in the oval of pale light, smoking.

Rae was walking stiffly and beginning not to breathe right, and she suddenly groaned in her chest. The man in the light looked at her but didn't move except to transfer his cigarette from his hand to his mouth. Quinn heard the liquid murmur of tires on bricks behind him, but he didn't want to look back. He stuck his pistol in his pants pocket, and held Rae more tightly.

As they approached under the light, the man looked over his shoulder, and Quinn saw he was the man who had shot Bernhardt. His features were the ones he had watched down the street a long way. The man's hair was across his forehead, and the poncho was gone and he was barefoot. When they came near him, the man turned and raised his hand and touched the brim of a hat he wasn't wearing and bowed slightly at the waist. He whispered something softly, the sound of a bee caught in a glass. The man was not out of his teens, and Quinn had the impulse to shoot him in the neck once and pay Bernhardt off for not bolting. The car coming against the traffic drifted noiselessly past the intersection. Quinn looked but it was not a police van, and then they were past the man at the light, looking onto the Avenue Juárez, which was masked and anonymous all the way down the hill toward the vapor lights in the Centro.

When they had walked ten meters, close to the store windows, Rae began to shake and then stopped walking. Her breathing became deep and quickened, and she sucked her tongue and pushed her head to the side as if she was going to be sick. He held her and pressed her shoulders against the window glass, and put his face close to hers for a long time, trying to join her breathing to his breathing, and calm her, staring through the cheap pane into an empty barbershop, at the chair and the white walls and the mirrors where he could see his reflection. And then by degrees he heard the soft suspiring night sigh of the city begin again, and Rae became erect and cool in his arms, and he could smell her breath hot and not sweet, and for a moment, with her close to him, his cheek on the cold glass, he felt himself fully located for once, and in a world in which time couldn't pass.

22

THEY WAITED INSIDE the shooting arcade behind the Juárez
Market. Teenagers were packed in, playing the games, drinking
the mescal, and yelling. There was the anxious smell of pomade
and the shabby, mesmerizing drowse of small chances being taken. Quinn stood at a machine on which a tall smiling Negress
in a red sari undressed as points went up, until only her red underpants were left and then they were gone and a cat's face smiled
in her crotch and lights flashed PUSSY, and the girl's expression
changed to an embarrassed *O*. He kept playing it until he couldn't
lose.

Rae sat on the wooden bench against the wall. Soldiers wandered in and stood in the door, lingering a moment considering
her, then walked back outside.

At midnight Quinn came and sat beside her. The popping,
clanging of the shooting games was loud and submerging, and he
tried just for a moment to hold things in place. Luck was infatuated with efficiency. But he couldn't work that trick now. He
thought about driving into St. Louis, headed overseas, about the
slow uneventful evening's ease of time out of Illinois and verging
on the realization of being nowhere at all that mattered. He took
a room downtown and walked up Olive Street to where the sun
was pink and gold, and the old brick warehouses relaxed in a

deep, slumbrous shadow. He remembered perfectly buying a cigar and two quarts of beer in a paper sack and walking down in the dusk to see the Cards, all so that he could not think for a time about going to Vietnam. A pressure seemed released and an inevitability forged, and he thought about the day with longing. And his mind now seemed to want that and nothing else.

"I'm over my head," Rae said, staring at the violet and yellow machines. Her voice was steady. She touched his hand with cold fingers.

"Let it go," he said. "You're flying out of here tomorrow."

She seemed not to hear. "Do you know that man who killed him?"

"No," Quinn said.

"Do you know who Carlos was calling?"

"I wouldn't guess."

She seemed removed from talk as if she was already gone. "Do we have any chances left?"

He stared at the Negress in her sari, waiting to be undressed. He wanted to play it again. "We're not even in it," he said.

"Can't you see Zago?"

"I can't think about him right now."

"If *you* aren't leaving . . ." she said and arranged her hands in her lap. "You used to say I made you feel lucky. Is that all gone now too?"

"I thought this was what I had to do to have you back."

"That's silly," Rae said. "It just seemed convenient."

He looked down the dark row of shooting games at the Mexican boys pouring money in. He reached in his pocket and felt his pistol. One of the children began banging on his machine and cursing in Spanish. The other players stopped and stared at him until he broke the glass on the machine. They all seemed fixed and detached in a pleasing way that made him want to stay in the gallery a long time.

"Let's get out of here," Rae said. "It reminds me of the dogs too much."

*

159

There were no more taxis, and the buses had quit at midnight. He led Rae up the Twentieth of November Street through the vegetable stands behind the market toward the zócalo. The streetlamps were off and a foreign blue light misted the air, stars pale and bristling above the alley openings. It made his mind clear. The Christmas lights were still lit in the zócalo, but the cafés in the Portal were shut and the metal tables stacked inside. He walked her across the empty park with his arm around her shoulders. The Baskin-Robbins had been boarded and the soldiers patrolling the Centro were inattentive or asleep on their feet.

The dining tables he had seen from Bernhardt's car were still lined across the hotel atrium. The clerk stood behind the high desk listening to a radio and rolling dice with himself. He looked at them as though he'd seen them before but didn't care. Quinn said in Spanish that there was a room and he wanted it. The clerk's look became drowsy, and he fingered a file in a drawer, then pulled a card. He studied the card awhile, as if he was trying to find what was wrong with it, then he smiled at Rae and laid the card on the desk top.

"No hay matrimoniales," he said proudly.

"What's that mean?" Rae said.

"No double beds." Quinn signed and gave the card back, waiting for the key.

"He thinks I'm a whore," she said and smiled at the clerk. "It must be these heels."

"It's a boring job," Quinn said, and put the key in his pocket.

The room was hot and full of flies and smelled like old laundry. Rae opened the window and stood for a moment looking without talking, as though she saw something in the distance over the low prospect of town that reassured her. Quinn pulled the transom, put his gun in the bureau drawer, and sat on the one wooden chair and watched the flies being soothed past Rae into the open night. In a while she took off her dress and lay on the bed beside the window in her white bra and underpants and the necklace he'd given her, and shut her eyes. Quinn turned on the bathroom light and checked the shower for scorpions, but there weren't any. He thought about the money up in the bungalow, but there was nothing he could do. It would keep there unless someone tore down the house. He washed his hands and walked back in the room.

Rae had begun to breathe steadily, her hair wide and deep red against the white covers.

He sat in the chair and watched her. He hadn't eaten in twenty-four hours, and hadn't had a pill in twelve. He was stronger than he thought he'd be and straight-headed. He watched Rae breathe until he heard steps in the hall approaching the room. Someone coughed, a man's voice, then keys jingled. He heard a lock fall, then the steps grew farther away and a door closed. He thought about Bernhardt, with every bullet in him as though he had danced to catch them all. He wondered if Cinco de Mayo was blocked off with trucks flashing lights, and soldiers sealing off the sidewalks. He imagined separate faces, Zago and Deats, but they seemed to lose ground irretrievably and be replaced by a vista over pale grey water, at the perimeter of which tiny dots didn't move, like boats too far out to picture. Bernhardt's absence made him feel marooned close to the clean, satisfied edge of exhausted possibility, beyond affection or sorrow, the stalemate edge of all losses, the point where time froze on whatever was present, and nothing could be longed for or feared or protected against, where luck was not the thing you played. It was the best luck there was. He might've liked Bernhardt, he thought, if he'd known him somewhere else. He had liked Bernhardt not always telling the truth, and not lying, and not leaving when he could've left. But that was it. He'd see Sonny one more time because he still had the responsibility to console. But he didn't love Sonny. And sometime in the afternoon he'd get on the plane with Rae, then that would be all that mattered anymore, an intimacy that didn't need an outside frame.

Rae stirred in the bed. Her legs parted and she moved on her side. Time seemed to expand around him and expectancy sub-

sided. He sat beside her on the bed and listened to her breathe
and watched her as though she was the only thing he could see.
He put his cheek on her side and felt the firm hits of her life.
Her flesh seized, and he knew she was cold, and he lay beside
her in his clothes and put his arms around her and held her to
try to make her warm.

23

At ten he walked across the Centro to the agency on Hidalgo Street. He had Rae's ticket validated and bought his own. The ticket was for nine in the morning. It gave him time to see Sonny and do what there was, and then get out. The connection went into New Orleans.

He walked back across the zócalo to where Rae was waiting at the taxi queue. He didn't want her at the bungalow now, but he didn't want her in the hotel either.

She stood in the fresh sunlight, looking up at the miradors circling the Centro as if they were a serious problem she didn't understand. She had on new blue sunglasses. "I know what's wrong here, Harry," she said.

"All of it's wrong," he said. He motioned for a cab. He wanted off the street. There were more tourists in town, and female students walking to the technological college in pairs. Things were resolving back to everyday enterprise. The Baskin-Robbins was still cordoned. The sky was wan and bluish, and the Christmas lights had been turned off, but the nearness to normal gave everything a delicacy that felt dangerous.

"There's just too much here that's uninteresting," she said, still studying the façades. "It isn't like Europe, I don't know why Sonny ever came here."

"He came to smuggle cocaine," Quinn said, pulling the cab door open. "I doubt if he had time for the sights."

"I guess that's right, isn't it?" she said and got inside.

✳

The cab passed up the Avenue Guerrero along the arts palacio. The side streets were crowded with tourists, and police vans were parked at the palacio gate, officers standing in the street waving machine guns. They were after stolen paintings, and Quinn put his window up. He wanted to get the money without an incident, then have what was left of the day to see Sonny and try to get a word to Zago. That was the only way he could plan it, and the money was crucial. He figured Deats worked for Zago creating dilemmas, since without Deats nothing changed in substance, but with him everything *seemed* desperate. But he didn't have to think about Deats anymore. Deats either had his troubles with Zago or he was off the case.

The cab turned up Manuel Ocampo three blocks off the zócalo, and there were soldiers massing. They were deployed on opposite sides of the street in the shadows, looking grey-faced and fidgeting. They had flak vests and riot visors, and had their weapons at sling-arms. Sergeants stood along the curb edges yelling into the lines and counting heads. The soldiers all wore new white canvas puttees below their GIs, and bright orange epaulettes. They were soldiers from somewhere else, with no qualms about shooting locals, since their own families couldn't be reached. And they were being hidden for a reason, something that would pop up suddenly, and where the usual anonymity wouldn't be enough.

The cab driver glanced at the soldiers. "Aéreos," he said and drove past cautiously. Rae fingered the window edge, gazing at the muster.

"What does that mean?" she said.

The only people he could see who were not soldiers were children hawking limes to the sergeants farther up the street. "Airborne," Quinn said.

"What are they doing?"

"Maneuvers." He kept his eyes on the direction the cab was going.

She took her glasses off and looked at him, her eyes white-lidded as though she had scrubbed them to get a stain off the skin. "I counted two hundred. That isn't good, is it?"

"Not our business," Quinn said.

She smiled. "We're different, right? Like Carlos said." She sat back around. "Hands to work. Hearts to God."

"Forget it," he said.

"I have a theory, you know." She was staring at the street. The cab had a painted tableau across the top border of its windshield, a long green pasture with a gold mountain in the distance and a black-haired girl with big tits in a bathing suit, standing at the edge of a lake smiling back into the cab. It gave the driver something to look at, and Rae stared past it as if she couldn't see it. "Women who marry older men are always grim," she said. "It's formulaic."

"You must have somebody in mind," Quinn said, watching the street.

"Zago's wife," Rae said.

"She's just another cunt, right?"

"She's worse," Rae said. "She's got busted luck all over her. You can smell it."

"I didn't notice," Quinn said.

"You're just not a woman," she said.

The cab passed a park where there was an oratory statue of Juárez wearing a concrete frock coat and a friar's hat. Something different from the deputy of penitentiaries' portrait. Juárez's devotees had littered the base with tall purple flowers, and there were two blue policemen standing beside a lone catalpa smoking and guarding the flowers. Beyond the park the houses were neat, pink and green mansionettes in arranged shady rows. All the likeness of Juárez made him be somebody else, somebody he wasn't, and Quinn thought that was his final good. He assumed nothing and risked everything, and when he was dead you could make him whatever you liked.

"Passion and melancholy get mixed up," Rae said, still musing about Zago's wife. "It's just a long funeral."

"Is that all your theory?" He was thinking about the bungalow, about getting into and out of it fast.

"That's why you're the way you are, Harry," she said and smiled at him.

"Fucked up, right?" he said. It annoyed him to get figured out, and figured wrong.

"You think you're always losing something," she said, "and you think you like to be alone, as if it made you powerful, but neither of those is true. That's all. I worry what would happen to you if I got killed."

"So do I," he said. "But that's so you won't have to."

"I don't mind," she said. "It makes me feel better. It ups the ante." She looked out at the genteel street. The cab had crossed the American Highway and started slowly up into the Reforma, where the houses were situated behind clean walls with citrus trees blooming over the tops. House servants were on the sidewalks pushing strollers.

"I guess I like the low odds better," he said.

"You *think* you do," she said. She was dreamy. "But you just want to be perfect, that's all, and justify everything you do. I'm not into that, I'm not that stupid. I'll take feeling good any way I can."

"You feel good now, do you?" he said and looked at her.

"Now I do," Rae said and smiled again. "Right now at this very moment, with all those soldiers, inside this cab, I do indeed. That's enough."

He thought of Bernhardt and regretted not to have regretted until now, but he'd been occupied.

"You're never ironic, Harry," she said airily. "That's really what's wrong with you. You need to be more ironic."

"Like you?" he said.

"Sure. Like me," she said and looked out the window again.
"I'm not so fucking bad."

*

The car was where he had left it. A good sign. It sat fifteen
meters below the bungalow gate beside a wall grown over with
bougainvillea and sky flowers. Two cars were farther up the hill,
a Renault and a red VW parked at the American girls' bungalow.
Two boys were setting firecrackers in the street and running, but
the street felt unattended.

Quinn watched through the windshield as the taxi eased up
Pinos Street, trying to notice anything out of the ordinary. The
air was cool and there was a new breeze on the hill not alive in
the Centro. The sense of openness reassured him.

"What's wrong?" Rae said. He had the pistol in his waistband.
He was set to light somebody up now. "Why are you looking so
strange?"

"Bad habits," he said. He thought about Bernhardt saying they
should be out of the house already.

The cab stopped at the gate. The driver turned and looked at
him. Something was making him nervous. "Espera momentito,"
Quinn said. It occurred to him to send Rae back down the hill
right now, but that was just as risky.

"What if somebody's inside?" she said, staring in at the bungalow.

"I want my fucking money," he said, and got out. He took the
gun out of his belt and cupped it. The metal door to the bungalow was open. He could see in through to the picture window that
gave on the city. Rae's blue Varig bag was lying in the yard, its insides yanked out. He picked it up and carried it to the door. The
boys in the street set off two firecrackers in quick succession, and
he could hear them laughing and their feet slapping pavement.

All the lights were on, the furniture was gone, and there was
a thin pane of brown water on the floor that stank. The house
seemed peaceful and enlarged, and it was empty.

167

He walked in through the bedroom. The bed and the table and his clothes were gone. In the bathroom the water was deeper. It seeped out below the toilet and flooded the shower trap with silt. Flies were humming on the ceiling.

He squatted behind the toilet and put the Varig bag and his pistol on the seat top. He could hear the taxi motor idling in the street. The smell was very grave, and the cesspool water soaked through his shoes. He hadn't thought about what had happened. But it was a given, something he could've figured out if he wanted to. He and Rae were simply not here anymore, and this was how you knew it.

The tiles behind the toilet were in place. He dug in the paste with his fingers and lifted, allowing the silt water to drain in the hole. He dug both hands in under the tiles and pulled the money bags out in two dripping handfuls and pushed them, tiles and all, into the Varig bag. The water had already filled the hole, and he saw where there was a deep crack in the porcelain from the base to the rim of the grail where somebody had kicked it. He wondered who did the kicking, and just exactly when, and then he heard Rae at the door. He zipped the Varig bag, picked up his gun, and went to the front where Rae stood, looking out over the sill. She stared at him oddly. "What *is* this?" she said. She almost smiled.

"Nothing. I've got the money," he said. Water was in his shoes. He wanted out of the bungalow. He pushed her backward out the doorway. He didn't know if Deats had done it, but Deats could get credit.

"Who did all this?" Rae said. She was holding on to the jamb, still looking inside, her face pale.

"Don't go in there," he said. The cab driver was trying to see them through the passenger window. He wanted to get out, and was staring at the pistol.

Rae suddenly grabbed his arm above the elbow and pulled it down. "Are they after us?"

"Get the fuck in the cab," he said. He put the Varig bag under his arm and pulled her toward the gate.

"Now just who did this?" she insisted, letting herself be pulled.

"It doesn't matter. I've got the fucking money."

The cab suddenly drove off down Pinos Street, leaving them in the open gate. The boys in the street were gone. Their papers fluttered on the pavement where they had been squatting.

"Was there somebody else inside?" she said loudly, pulling away.

"No. Forget that, just forget it," he said.

"Did you lose something important, Harry?" she said.

"No." He thought of the photograph of himself in the white sombrero smiling out at space. There was no record of that time's ever having taken place now.

"It's bad luck, isn't it?" Rae said, staring down the street at the empty Dodge parked against the bougainvillea wall.

"No," he said. "It doesn't mean anything. Get in the car." And he pushed her down the street toward the Dodge.

24

AT THE HOTEL there was a message at the administración.
The lobby was full of German tourists in walking shorts with
Swiss suitcases on wheels, trying to speak in English to the day
clerk who seemed offended and was shaking his head no. The
Germans wanted out of their reservations, and they were shouting that the town was dangerous now. They stared at Quinn when
he took his message, and started yelling again when he didn't offer to help.

Rae stood at the window in the room watching the zócalo while
he read the note. Students from the technological college had begun a demonstration in the park. He could hear bursts of exhor-
tative Spanish shouted through a bullhorn, followed by cries of
approval from the people who had gathered. The bursts concerned
the police, and then fighting to the end of something, but he
couldn't understand the rest. He remembered the soldiers lined
along Manuel Ocampo, and the paper posters on the fronts of
the shanties where the Mexican boy had been dead. They didn't
matter now.

He put the letter on the table and thought about a place for
the money. Every place was obvious, though there wasn't any
pure reason to think anyone wanted it anymore, if they ever had.

Rae picked up the note and read it standing at the table. It was in letters printed with a black sketching pen. It said:

Mr. Harry Quinn,
I see your problem, and I can help you with it. I'll drive to pick you up at eight o'clock. No compromisos.

Susan Zago

Rae put the letter on the tabletop and walked back to the window and looked out. "Are you going?" she asked. Her voice was taut. There was a loud shout of appreciation and some applause from the demonstration. Someone yelled "God damn it" into the bullhorn, and there was applause.

"No," Quinn said. He stood in the middle of the room still imagining a place for the money. "Unless I have to," he said.

"Why would you *have* to?"

"I don't know. I don't have any goddamn idea why I'd have to." He sat on the bed beside the Varig bag. "Sonny's just got to play it straight now. No more fucking around."

"Are you going to see him?" she said.

"I can get in at four if everything's all right."

"You mean if somebody hasn't killed him?" He looked at her without speaking, his hand on the money bag. "What about Zago?" she said. She wasn't going to lose it again. She was reliable, and there wouldn't be any more slips.

"I'll call him. I'll go out in the car. Whatever. I just want to try to get him out."

"I'd rather not go to the prison today," she said. She blinked as though she'd said something he hadn't heard. She came and knelt at the foot of the bed, staring at the chalky tiles.

"You just might not see him again," Quinn said. It didn't matter. But he wanted to go through it to the end.

"You know," she said, kneeling, talking with animation. "I dropped my necklace this morning while you were getting the tickets, and do you know what I found when I picked it up?" She didn't look at him, looked closely at the floor.

He watched her without answering. She was trying to smile. "Somebody had written in pencil on this floor, 'Flint, Michigan, 194,000 population, Automobiles, A wonderful place to live.'" She looked up at him oddly, her hair in her face. "I thought those dead people were in this room. It made me cry because we were going to get out and they weren't." Tears were in her eyes, and she began to rub out the writing with her hand. "Just say I'm sorry," she said and shook her head.

He said, "Do you want to take a cab ride down to Mitla?"

"I'm going to sleep now," she said. She sat beside him on the bed, tears on her face. "Why do you think Bernhardt ditched her?" she said.

"I could come up with some reasons," he said.

She put her hands in her lap and stared at the open window. "You can't depend on somebody who's on the ropes. He must've been smart enough to know that. He just wasn't smart enough to know what to do about it."

"Maybe he loved her."

"Don't say that, Harry," she said.

"Is that the other half of your theory?" He picked up the Varig bag.

"You can't depend on somebody who's on the ropes," she said accusingly.

"What about me?" Quinn said. "Can you depend on me?"

"I don't know about you," she said. "It's fucked up where you're concerned."

"I already said that. But I could put you on a bus tonight," he said. "I don't care."

"Just go fuck," she said, crying. "I don't have any place to go. If I did, I would, but I don't."

"I'll be back then," he said.

25

IN THE LOBBY the Germans were sitting against the wall behind their suitcases-on-wheels. They looked resentful. They watched him at the desk as though they suspected he was being given privileges they weren't allowed to have anymore.

Quinn wanted the money in the lockup. There was no good place for it, so the obvious had become practical. The clerk took the bag and gave him the box key without showing him the fit, then asked him in English if he was interested in a tour of Monte Albán. He said no and asked for the phone. The clerk seemed annoyed and led him into the office where the lock boxes were, and where the air had stale smoke in it. The Germans watched cynically when he went behind the desk and began whispering. The clerk handed him a directory and disappeared into the lobby.

He wanted to tell Zago the deal was still on, and deliver what Zago wanted as quick as he could get it. The document of release expired in two days, and a lawyer would have to get another one. So it was impossible to start over now. The best that was left was to keep Sonny alive. There wasn't time to get him out.

No one answered at the first Luis Zago, and he dialed the

next, watching the door to the lobby. He could hear the Germans mumbling and the clerk's feet scuffing the tile floor. In the park there were shouts from the demonstration.

The voice that answered spoke in English. He hadn't expected it, and he waited a moment, thinking. He wanted to speak Spanish, but Zago's wife would know who it was.

"Let me speak to Luis Zago," he said quickly.

"He's not here," Zago's wife said.

He kept his eyes on the door for a sign of the clerk. "Do you expect him?"

"Is this Mr. Quinn?"

"I need to talk to your husband pretty bad. Can I talk to him?" he said. He felt stupid. The Mexican telephone was stupid, and he felt like a tourist calling home for help.

"He's out of town, Mr. Quinn. He won't be back for a week." She paused a moment. "Am I going to see you tonight?" She sounded amused.

The idea that Zago was unreachable opened like a lightless room. He understood she was lying, but it didn't matter if he couldn't get to Zago right away. Bernhardt had been the only contact, and he was out of it. He wondered for the first time who had killed Bernhardt and why they'd bother. "No," he said.

"Maybe you'll change your mind," she said. "There're no obligations."

"Just tell me how can I reach your husband," he said.

"I don't think he wants to see you anymore," she said cheerfully. "But I do."

"Forget it," he said, and put down the receiver.

✳

In the lobby the Germans were gone and Rae stood in the middle of the lobby, crying. "I was waiting for you to come out on the street, and you didn't come," she said. "I thought something happened to you." She began walking back toward the stairs.

"I made a call," he said.

174

She was sobbing. "Then you should tell me, God damn it."

He put his arms around her at the bottom of the stairs. There was a cheer out in the park. "It's all right," he whispered in her ear.

"No it's not," she said. Her hair was damp and smelled stale. He took the lock-box key and put her hand on it.

"This is the bag," he said softly. He turned and looked across the lobby for the clerk, but no one was behind the desk. The lobby was deserted, though a waiter in a white jacket stood in the atrium scalding glasses in a pan of water for the comida. All the tables had white cloths on them, and the light was watery. He could hear the glasses tinkling. "It's behind the desk," he said.

"Are you getting us in trouble now?" she said, still facing the dim marble stairs up to the room. Her voice was accusing.

"No way," he said.

"I wish you wouldn't," she said. "I've really had enough now." She began the stairs without looking back at him.

✳

There were no buses on the highway and few cars that weren't heading south toward Chiapas. The Germans had seemed to want to leave town in a hurry, and that was a bad sign. Up in the mountains the sky was bruising up to rain, and he could see the pale curtains distinctly farther down the valley. The south had a wide, softened prettiness in the rain light, and the entire landscape seemed to be under a different authority, as if it had become familiar. The children who sold iguanas were gone, their adobe empty and ruined. One iguana was left strung to the electric pole, hanging motionless in the cool sunlight.

The army inspection had been reinforced. He recognized none of the faces, but none of the soldiers had white puttees or orange epaulettes. There was a bivouac behind the wood shelter with tents set up in facing rows. There were two new six-by-sixes and another sixty bagged to face toward town. When he drove in under the awning, the soldiers manning the sixty swiveled the target irons slowly toward the windshield and stared impassively. There were no cars at the inspection, and the corporal took his turista card inside the shelter, copied something onto a clipboard and showed it to another soldier, then returned it without comment. When he drove back out onto the road the soldier wrote down his license number. It was all routine and unimportant, but it made him think about the Americans at the airport and what they saw at the end that probably seemed routine. Maybe just a jeep, or a soldier holding a light, or someone waving. There was never any way to get spared, then, no way for anyone to know what you were doing or where you were. Everything was bad risk. It all screwed down to make you feel as far away as possible from anything that cared about you.

✳

He sat alone in the visitation, facing the yellow door. The cafeteria had the same sweet urine stink from the day before, though it was empty except for the guards at either end. The visiting hour was nearly over and the guards were bored and careless. Water had seeped from the walls and the pools were full of dead beetles. Outside someone was methodically kicking a ball against concrete.

When Sonny stepped into the room, he had a wide gauze bandage on his head that was thick over his left ear. His hair had been cut to his scalp and his face looked too white. He looked as if he wasn't sure where he was, and might cry but didn't want to.

"Did they let you see medics?" Quinn said automatically, when Sonny was in front of him. He pushed the Gauloises pack across the table. He wasn't sure Sonny could speak, and that was everything now. "What in the fuck happened?" He rested his hands on the table. He wanted to take Sonny's hand, but he didn't want to be conspicuous. Someone continued kicking the ball outside.

176

"My ear," Sonny said softly. Tears suddenly swelled out, and he shut his eyes and pressed his lips against his teeth.

He wasn't sure he could make Sonny understand, though he thought the situation had to be pretty clear. "Now listen," he said, "they know you skimmed it." He glanced at the two guards who were watching Sonny oddly.

Sonny looked dazed. He seemed to want to portray disappointment but didn't know how. "What's going to happen, Harry?" he whispered. He raised his hand to touch his ear, then put it back under the table.

"Did you hear what the fuck I said? You've got to give it back, or they're going to blow you up."

Sonny's blue eyes blinked. "Who?" he said.

"Zago."

Sonny shook his head and smiled. "I don't know *him*," he said. His eyes glazed as if words were in his head but wouldn't get organized and he was waiting for them to do that. "Two guys came in to cut my hair last night, you know. They said I was coming out. Then they took scissors and cut off my ear."

"Zago did it," Quinn said. "You've gotta quit this shit. You understand?"

Sonny blinked again. His eyes looked like Rae's eyes expressing something he'd seen Rae express, bewilderment over too much at once. "I didn't lay any shit off, Harry," Sonny said in a practiced voice. He let his gaze drop to the Gauloises box. "I picked it up in the room. I took a cab. Some dudes in white shirts came in the airport and grabbed me and I got set up." He let his eyes wander slowly toward the exit at the far end of the cafeteria. "Where's Bernhardt?" He stared at the yellow door as if he thought Bernhardt was going to walk through it.

"Look, God damn it." He grabbed Sonny's hands and squeezed. He didn't want to freak him. "Why would they think you did it if you didn't do it?" he said softly. "This is just business, O.K.? It's all business."

Sonny stared at him. His pupils were wide and deep. He felt

like he could see inside Sonny's brain. "Maybe," Sonny said, "somebody's fooling somebody else. That's been done, hasn't it, Harry?" Sonny smiled. He moved his hand again toward his ear, then stopped halfway and put his hands on the table, and began to move his head down toward where his hand was. "My ear doesn't hurt," he said. "They gave me a shot. I don't feel it."

"Why get me in this, God damn it?" He felt desperate, though it wasn't an unsatisfying feeling, just a familiar one, almost a calming one.

"It *looks* good," Sonny said very softly, almost muttering.

"To who? Who gives a shit?"

"Maybe they had an argument, you know," Sonny said. He couldn't keep his head still and his eyes began to rove. Whoever had been kicking the ball had stopped, and the absent noise hollowed the silence in the cafeteria. Sonny's blood stream was loading up now. "You know, Harry," he said. "I had a dream this morning. I was standing by my Cadillac, holding a basketball, and there was a hedge beside it and a field with some woods in it. And the trunk of the car was all full of my shit, and there were four hats. And somehow some Mexicans came up and took the hats and put them on and started to leave. And I said, 'Those are my hats, man,' and they said, 'We're Mexicans, you don't own anything.'" Sonny smiled. "And that was all. I didn't argue. Though I thought they were doing something wrong. And they stayed out in the field where I could see them, wearing my hats." His smile widened.

"Please cut this shit out," Quinn said and looked down. Both guards were watching him strangely. One glanced at his wrist watch and said something to the other one, and both looked at him again. "Dionisio's dead, man. Carlos is dead. This shit is up. They're all over you."

Sonny stared intently at the box of Gauloises, his eyes bright. He seemed frustrated but not even aware of it. "You know," he said, "it's a goddamn good feeling to fuck somebody you don't know." He looked up proudly, as if he'd discovered something wonderful.

"Why *is* that?" Quinn said.

Sonny smiled. Someone started kicking the ball again, the hits popping as if there was a hurry. "Well," he said slowly, and grew silent again. "If you start finding out things the next thing you know she's saying, 'Why don't we do it as much as we used to?' And then you're all set up, you can't do anything, and you're out of control, you understand? You don't want to be there, do you?" Sonny took a deep breath and held Quinn's hands and squeezed them. "If you don't know anything though, Harry, you can fuck her till piss turns to Popsicles and everything's great. That's where I made my mistake with Kirsten, you know, I found out too much, tried too hard." He smiled. Flies were on his bandage. Sonny was sweating out of enthusiasm for the idea he had in his head. It kept him from being afraid. In whatever way, Quinn thought, that he was like Sonny, he hoped he had better ideas.

"I know what you did," Quinn said softly. "Can't you just tell me where you put it?"

"What is this man?" Sonny said. "Tell me what you're talking about, Harry? Where I put what?" Quinn looked up at the guards, who were walking toward him. "I'm really fucked up," Sonny said, smiling and looking relaxed. "I know you're saying shit I'm not understanding. You'll have to come back, you know. Maybe tomorrow."

"O.K.," Quinn said and stood up to leave. "You try to get it right tomorrow."

A fly lit on Sonny's hand, and he slowly let his other hand cover it. "You gotta kill these fucking flies, man," Sonny said. "They'll keep you awake." He smiled.

26

ON THE TWENTIETH of November Street it had begun to rain. The daylight was used up and water was bouncing off the bricks in front of the taxis, trickling into a garbage current along the gutters. The pottery alleys on Bustamante were open, and a few tourists in rain gear had avoided the army barricades and were walking the slick streets through the rain. Two German men in walking shorts stood under an umbrella, pointing to a particular stall where candelabra were sold. The clerk waited at the verge of the lighted shed yelling at them, beckoning in the mist.

Quinn's stomach exerted a failing low-grade pain he thought would quit if he didn't concentrate on it. He hadn't eaten in a long time, and this was only a minor flare-up. He thought it could be nerves, a bad reaction to Sonny letting go.

He walked up the line of pottery stalls across from the Hotel Señoria, examining the green fish dishes and black cups in straw paper, wanting something to catch his eye. Coming back empty-handed was going to leave Rae with the day empty and nothing to connect with. It wasn't kind enough. He came to a stall selling the purple flowers he had seen piled around Juárez's statue. The Indian woman was shouting "heliotropos" into the street and he bought a paper full and started back to the hotel in the rain.

He felt hollowed out now and he tried to think if Bernhardt

had mentioned anybody, relatives he could call. He had said once he had a wife somewhere who hadn't worked out, and a mother, but there was no way to find them now in time, no way to express perfunctory sympathy. It was as if Bernhardt never existed. His constancy had simply leached away. Bernhardt and Deats were beginning to take equal importance in his mind, and that seemed incorrect but impossible to change.

When he reached the Centro, the demonstrators who had been in the park were gone. The soldiers in white puttees from Manuel Ocampo were patrolling the empty sidewalks in the rain. Leaflets littered the promenades, and the cathedral floodlights had been turned on, making the drizzle spectral in the dense light. The soldiers still wore their riot visors and moved self-consciously through the water, their guns at order. The zócalo itself seemed orderly and private, and the few tourists in the cafés in the Portal had their backs to the streets, as if whatever was in the arcade was what they had expressly come to see.

He called the American consulate from the hotel office. He wanted every chance used. Bernhardt had explained it to him carefully. Bad shit in the prisión was what the consulate went to sleep on, and if he couldn't prove Sonny was about to take an egregious down, no one would pay attention. But it was last chance time. The phone rang and rang then was answered by a recording of a man's voice with a Boston accent that sounded, itself, like a recording. He recognized the voice from the first day he saw lawyers, a man named Benson. Benson's voice said to leave a number and a message and someone would call back. He tried Zago's number but no one answered, and he walked on up the stairs with the heliotropes wetting his hands.

✳

"Something happened outside," Rae said. She was standing with her back to the open window. Her face was rigid.

"I guess," he said. He put the heliotropes in the pure-water bottle and set it on the chair.

"No, you don't guess," she said tightly. "Something bad

happened. It scared everybody. And you don't look scared." She wound her hands. "I went to sleep and I dreamed shooting and people getting killed, and when I woke up all those soldiers we saw were out there, and the students were gone. Did you see that?"

"No." He sat on the bed and watched her with the rain hissing like a curtain in the early dark. He tried to remember the shooting for her sake.

"The police came up here," she said. She looked betrayed, as if there was a blame she wanted assigned.

His mind raced to his pistol and then to the money in the lock box. He stood up and went to the bureau and opened the second drawer. "What'd they say?" The pistol was gone.

"They said they were thinking of arresting me," Rae said. "I saw them drive up in the street, and I hid your gun. I don't know why I knew they were coming."

He looked around the room. "Where is it?" he said.

"On the ledge."

He leaned out into the rain and felt the pistol on the string course. No one on the street looked up. "Did they mention Carlos?" he said.

Rae sat on the bed watching him. "Often."

He wiped the gun on his pants. "What happened?"

He opened the breech to check for water.

"I told them Señor Bernhardt was our lawyer. I told them we had to see him tomorrow, and I told them I wanted them to leave because I didn't feel well." She looked up at him with no expression.

"What did they say?" He pushed the cylinder closed and put the gun back in the drawer. There wasn't any water.

"That he was muerto," Rae said. "That must mean dead."

He looked at her. "Did they think you were surprised?"

"I tried," she said, "but they were rude about it. It made me mad."

"What else?" He began to try to figure what it meant that the

182

police had come at all, if it meant they were checking all Bernhardt's clients. Everything seemed to have four dimensions now. It was hard to concentrate right. It was like an illness.

"That's all," Rae said. "I went down and checked the lock box. They know something about us now, Harry." She seemed fatigued.

"There's nothing to know." He looked out the window at the other arcade of the Portal. Absence of people made the buildings seem distinct and depthless in the rain. The Christmas lights had been turned on, but the band kiosk was empty, except for a soldier in the shadows. "We haven't done a goddamned thing," he said. It made him mad she was conceding a thing she didn't have to. It was something entirely different from giving Sonny up.

"I think they just haven't figured out why they should arrest us yet," she said calmly. "I don't think it matters what you do, it's whether they think they should arrest you."

"That's wrong," he said. "You're wrong about that. We didn't kill anybody."

"Did Sonny tell you where he put it?"

"No, he didn't."

"Has he been lying to us?"

"Sure." His mind began to race, then stopped at nothing.

Rae lay back on the bed. "So are they going to kill him?"

"I have to think yes," he said. "Zago's not answering his phone. I called the consulate. They're calling me back." She knew everything important now. They were looking at the same picture. "I didn't think Zago'd back out," he said.

"No fixed ideas," Rae said, and looked at him. "Sonny's luck just ran out, didn't it, Harry? That's why I didn't go today. I didn't want to come in behind that."

Quinn thought about drinking beers in San Pedro, and Sonny saying he'd rather be in business. That didn't seem so long ago.

"There's no use calling the consulate if you don't have anything to say, is there?" she said.

"I can say he's alive." He looked at her. "I want to stay with that if I can. He's supposed to survive this. That's why I'm here."

He thought about Susan Zago. The nonsensical always became the thinkable once you reached the logical flash point. The war was that way. At some point it just became more interesting to think about the deviances.

"He's just an asshole jock," Rae breathed and closed her eyes. "He's not salvageable. He's like me."

"You love him, though, right?" he said, staring at her. "That makes you salvageable."

"I hate him," she said.

"That'd probably surprise him," Quinn said. She was putting up perimeters now, something he couldn't quite do. He could always see anybody's problem if the payoff was big enough. It was a shit way to operate.

The cathedral clock began chiming six.

"I don't hate him to punish him," Rae said earnestly and raised on her elbows. "Do you understand that? I hate him so I can *not* feel bad. I'll feel bad later, but I'll be with you then. If I felt bad now I don't know if I could stand to be with you anymore." She smiled. Somebody had to feel bad, and if it was her he was going to lose. But if it was him, that was just the standard price. "What're you about to do?" she said. She looked at the purple heliotropes on the chair as if they had been in the room all along.

"See Zago's wife," he said.

Rae looked at him oddly. "That's a bum idea."

He sat opposite her on the bed. "I already heard that."

"But you didn't pay attention, Harry," she said. She looked at him as if she saw something perplexing. "She's a down-and-outer."

He put his hands on her legs. "That's right." He felt better being near her, his mind sliding off center. He didn't need to hear what she said.

"She killed Carlos because he ditched her," Rae said dreamily. "That's right, isn't it?"

He could feel the long muscles lengthen up her thighs and then, by inches, relax. She didn't have the wish to resist now. Importance was slipping away, and she would give it all over to him.

She lay on her back and let him touch her. He could hear her breath subside and shallow. He felt dead-even on everything. "Did you bring me those flowers?" she said. She was staring sideways. The room smelled like rain. He could hear the hiss off the street, and in the distance a voice in conversation he couldn't understand. "I noticed them, you know, but I didn't know where they came from. I decided they'd been here all along, and I'd overlooked them." She reached for him. "I must be going crazy," she said. "I don't seem to feel anything right anymore." She looked at him as if they were inside something she couldn't find her way back from and was ready now to hear the thing she was supposed to do.

27

QUINN STOOD OUT OF THE RAIN under the hotel marquee. Cafés in the Portal were half-empty, Americans sitting resolutely in their tin folding chairs drinking Tecates and staring back into the restaurants where the lights were blue and cold. The soldiers on the square slouched into the lees of buildings, and the police stood behind the Baskin-Robbins' sawhorses, yawning at the dark.

He had called the consulate and gotten the same recording and the story didn't seem solid anymore. Sonny'd had a breakdown. Nobody'd believe it soon enough. They thought about Sonny, he realized, the way you thought about somebody's grandmother in South Dakota whose life was interesting and then absolutely forgettable, so that there wasn't even a way to specify what Sonny suffered or might end up suffering. He felt like he had gained more precision but lost more accuracy, which seemed ridiculous, the opposite of experience. The rain hung in the air. He listened to the blue neon hum, stared at the darkness, and tried to believe he could still work it. He had the pistol, but he didn't have a waterproof for the rain.

A Renault turned off the Avenue Morelos and idled along the north term of the zócalo, disappearing, then reappearing behind its headlights at the corner. The soldiers watched it as dismally as they watched the rain. The Renault passed the colonnade of the government palacio, then turned up the Twentieth of November Street to the hotel and stopped, water shining and hitting noisily off the windshield.

The driver's window came half-down. Susan Zago's white face looked out at him, her features more purposeful than the night before. Her eyes were alive and attentive. "Please get in," she said.

✳

"Where's this going?" Quinn said when the car was moving. He checked the back seat—too late, he realized—but there was no one there. It was unsafe, like not noticing the moza had been in the bungalow.

Susan Zago was wearing a rubber mackintosh and was regarding the streets as if she was following a route that was hard to make out. She seemed animated. Her hair had been tied back and she was wearing perfume. "I have to see if I'm followed," she said.

"Who'd follow you?" he said.

"My husband. The police." She glanced in the rearview. "They don't like my friends."

"Don't you think they know exactly what you do?" he said.

"Maybe," she said and smiled. "You can always think everything's on a grid and somebody's responsible for everything. But it isn't true."

"What do you think *is* true?"

"No one cares," she said. "It's like every place else, unless they've got money in it, of course. You just don't know where they have money."

She headed toward the American Highway by the brightly lit Pemex where the overland trucks were lined up to refuel in the rain, then through the Zapata rotary and back in toward the Centro along the second-class bus route. Suddenly she turned the car sharply onto a residential street that ended in a block in a park full of trees with their trunks painted white like the trees in the zócalo. She stopped at the curb and closed the lights. No other car came off the avenue, but she sat watching the mirror as though she expected to see something. It was play-acting. He thought he ought to try to get out now and back to the hotel as quick as he could. Only he didn't want to be in the street with the gun. "Your wife is certainly pretty," Susan Zago said, watching the mirror all the time.

"Let's goddamn get on with this," he said.

Susan Zago restarted the car. "It's not me you're seeing," she said.

"I guessed," he said.

"My friends don't want to be surprised," she said, still watching the glass. Animation made her prettier than she'd seemed before.

"Who killed Bernhardt?" he said. He realized he wanted to know and this was the right place to find out.

"I have no idea," Susan Zago said airily. She made a U-turn in the street and approached the wide avenue slowly in the dark. "He was narco-tráfico," she said. "A lot of people might have killed him. There was probably a queue."

"I don't think so," Quinn said.

"It doesn't much matter what you think," she said.

"It was your husband, right?"

She turned on the lights and eased into the avenue. She seemed impressed that she was doing things right. "Why should he?" she said.

"Because of the kind of photography you and Carlos used to tease each other."

"He doesn't care about that," she said, her face motionless in the dash light. "It's not your business anyway. Who I fuck is my business."

"It was supposed to make me trust him."

"How nice," she said. She seemed amused, as if Bernhardt

had been a child she was tired of. "Are you happy you trusted him?"

"You said it." He watched her face in the dark. He wanted to see a response. "It's my business. It didn't work out, that's all."

"Apparently not." She turned down Bustamante Street above the Centro, where there were no streetlights. "But it leaves you in a bad position now, I'm afraid," she said.

There were no soldiers on the street, and the pottery alleys in the next block were shut, though far down beyond the market he could see in the sheen of night rain the glare of the truck garages still working.

"I want to know who Deats is," Quinn said. They were not very far from the Hotel Monte Albán. He thought he could make it back all right now and he felt safer, which he knew was also silly.

"He's a man who works for my husband," Susan Zago said, carefully watching the adobe façades pass by the car window. She was looking for something that required her concentration. "In the States. You know? A connection?" She looked at him as though she'd figured something out. "You need time, don't you Mr. Quinn? But you don't have it. Too many facts piling up."

"I guess I'll have to brave it," he said.

She stopped the Renault outside a white building without windows, but with a curved arch-entry to an invisible inside. It became quiet a moment. "I always try to remember everything that ever happened to me, you know?" She smiled over at him appealingly, her face pale and calm. Her perfume smelled sweet. "So I need time. I suppose I think everybody else is the same way."

"I forget as much as I can," Quinn said.

"A tough guy," she said, and her look became strange again, as if she believed him and pitied him at the same time.

"How did you get into this?" he said.

"In what?" she said.

"These people."

"It's fun," she said, and looked out the window behind him into the rain as if for a signal. "Don Luis is an old man. I'm interested in young men. Our interests coincide." She opened her door. "There's nothing else amusing to do here."

The arch-entry protected them a moment from the rain, then opened to an atrium where there was a low concrete sculpture and a reflecting pool. The building was two-tiered with a loggia and a stone staircase at the far end that rose to the gallery level. The rain was intense inside the court, and it was hard to see what the sculpture was imitating.

Susan Zago hurried up the far stairs ahead of him and Quinn had a strong feeling suddenly of being followed. He looked back in the open court, but no one was there.

At the top of the stairs a man leaned forward out of the dark with a short, blunt-nosed weapon, and Susan Zago immediately stepped aside. The man was not a man really, but the boy who had killed Bernhardt. He was wearing thick black-rimmed glasses with wet lenses, and put the barrel of the gun squarely in the middle of Quinn's stomach and reached forward to search. "Don't cause trouble," Susan Zago said quietly from the side. "This is necessary."

He wanted to concentrate on the boy. He had almost shot him the night before and now the same boy was keeping him in the rain while he patted under both arms and down his trouser seams, the gun barrel jerking against his stomach. The boy smelled like disinfectant and didn't search like Zago's man. He did it the way he'd seen it in movies, and he missed the pistol in the small of his back. The boy's hair was wet and parted in the middle and slicked back, making him look very young. When he finished the boy dropped his eyes. It felt odd, Quinn thought, always to be intimate with strangers, never with people you cared about. Kids with guns. Ladrinos. It had to be another phase of the modern predicament.

He wanted to know how many people were here now. It was a measure of normal efficiency to know who you're going to see coming back out. He looked around the dark gallery, but there was no one to see behind the other balusters.

Midgallery there was a door to the right. Susan Zago stopped in front and turned. "You get to see where I paint," she said. Her skin was light colored and her hair shone in the dark.

"Who's that boy?" he said. He touched the pistol grip, found he could reach it with his entire hand. He felt himself getting cold along his ribs.

"Just a boy," she said. "Do you know him?"

" 'Fraid not," he said.

"Just step inside," she said.

The air inside made him think there were high ceilings, though he couldn't see walls. The air felt cool and large, and there was a thin odor like kerosene that didn't seem to come from any one direction. Susan Zago closed the door and shut out the rain noise, and immediately there was a sound to the left of feet moving. He couldn't see distinctly. Water ran out of his hair, and he pulled the gun to the front of his belt against his stomach.

There was the sound of glass scraped over metal, and a match flared low to the floor. He could see two knees and two hands raising the chimney of a metal lantern. The odor of kerosene grew stronger while the man fingered the glass, holding the match until the wick flamed and burnt off freshly and began a glow. The man lowered the chimney with his finger tips, adjusted the jet so the light grew into the dark, then picked up the lantern and held it out and walked forward toward where Quinn stood with Susan Zago.

"This is Señor Muñoz," Susan Zago said formally.

He watched the man shape up behind the lantern. He was a tall handsome boy in his twenties with a smooth brown face and fine features that looked more intelligent than the boy's outside. He was wearing a blue cotton work shirt and white pants, and his hair was neat. His eyes moved confidently to Susan Zago when he heard his name spoken. He had a big automatic pistol stuck in the front of his trousers, the grip turned toward the hand that carried the lantern. When he came closer he raised the lantern so that Quinn could feel the heat in his eyeballs, then drew it back as if he had satisfied himself. "I am sorry to meet you this way," the boy said politely, and his face became serious. "I would like to meet you in a nice restaurant if I could. But." He smiled in an embarrassed way.

Quinn tried to think if this was a boy he'd seen her with in the Portal. "This'll do," Quinn said. "Let's just get on with it."

Muñoz's eyes darted at the ceiling, then back as if he had avoided saying something. Quinn could see high on the walls, but not low. They were white with no windows, though most of the studio felt behind him. The lantern hissed and Muñoz took a firm breath. "Your brother is in the cárcel?" he said softly.

"Right," Quinn said.

Muñoz's eyes trained on him thoughtfully. "It is a terrible place," he said.

"In a world of bad places," Quinn said.

Muñoz thought a moment, then smiled appreciatively. "Is true. But I can bring him out for you. It is not difficult."

"That's odd," Quinn said, "because it's been really difficult for me so far. You understand?"

"My brother is the guardia," Muñoz said with authority. Muñoz was a student. He had that bullshit unassailable certainty about him. "So it is possible to let your brother out," he said, "and to take him where it is safe." Muñoz's eyes held steady. You couldn't know what that steadiness meant, except he was eager.

"Where's safe?" Quinn said.

"Las montañas," Muñoz said. "Hay muchas lugares. There are many places safe there." Muñoz looked confidentially at Susan Zago.

"What do *you* want?" Quinn said.

Susan Zago translated.

"Money," Muñoz said, and looked serious.

"How much?" Quinn said.

"In dólares," Muñoz said. He paused a moment to think. "Five thousand," he said firmly. "There is the risk. It is more."

"When would it take place?" he said.

"You don't have time to wait, do you?" Susan Zago said abruptly. She stepped out of the dark.

"I'll find time," he said.

"Esta noche," Muñoz said quickly.

"And I pay when he's out, right?" He guessed the answer, but he wanted to hear it.

"No," Muñoz said emphatically. "You pay now." He blinked several times.

"Half. And half when he's safe," Quinn said.

Muñoz looked at Susan Zago oddly, as though he had failed a connection. She spoke something in quick Spanish, and Muñoz held the lantern higher so that the kerosene smell became richer. "You must trust us," Muñoz said. His eyes flickered but he wasn't angry. "I will show you." Muñoz stepped past into the dark half of the studio.

Quinn was aware of the rain beating on a skylight at the end of the room. Muñoz stepped toward the far wall, holding the lantern up, until the yellow began to illuminate something unusual he could only partly see. Muñoz came near whatever it was and the light clarified a shape wrapped in clear plastic, leaned against a wood chair. Behind the chair several framed canvases were stacked against the wall. One he could see was of a terrace overlooking a harbor with pennants flying at the edge of the blue water.

"See," Muñoz said, and pulled away the plastic. Deats was in the chair. Muñoz folded the plastic so that Deats' head was exposed. A purple bump spoiled the middle of Deats' smooth forehead. His eyes were half-open, and his arms had been tied back with cloth, and blood had come out his nose and run into his mouth. Muñoz stared at Deats appraisingly, then looked up at Quinn with confidence. "Es Señor Deats," he said in a proud whisper. He held the lantern near Deats' face so that the light made Deats' khaki skin shine, then held it up again in the dark.

"You're showing this to the wrong customer," Quinn said. Deats wasn't different from any other dead man, just nothing there. But he didn't want to look at Deats again, and the entire room seemed different, as if it had suddenly become too familiar.

"It's what you paid for," Susan Zago said flatly. "It's what Carlos was arranging for you."

"Sometimes it is necessary to kill someone," Muñoz said, standing holding the lantern. "So you must trust us now," he said.

He realized everyone was offering pledges of steadfastness all of a sudden. "Let's just get the fuck on with this." He turned back to Muñoz.

"Pay us now," Muñoz said. He held the lantern in front of him. "It is business."

"You bet," Quinn said.

Susan Zago said something in Spanish. Muñoz stopped walking and frowned at her as if she had suggested something that insulted him. He looked at Quinn, then reached suddenly for his pistol with the lantern hand. The glass chimney swagged his leg and the bail caught the hammer, and Muñoz peered down at it oddly as if he didn't understand the mechanics of it. Quinn already had his gun in both hands, pointing at Muñoz's shirt pocket. The lantern jigged up and down as Muñoz carefully unclasped the bail from the hammer.

"Don't do that," Quinn yelled. He couldn't think of the right Spanish words and it made him feel stupid, as if he wasn't going to be able to make the boy understand before he had to shoot him.

"No, no," Susan Zago said. She extended both hands, palms out. Her face was panicky. "Basta, querido mio," she said. She looked at Quinn beseechingly. "He's just a baby," she said. "He isn't doing this right, please. You haven't given him a chance."

Muñoz looked up at her and pursed his lips tightly. Her alarm seemed to disappoint him, and he looked womanly, like someone caught impersonating a man.

"Tell him just leave the fucking gun alone," Quinn yelled. He heard footsteps outside and squeezed on the grips. Muñoz stared at the pistol pointing at him, then raised his own slowly. "Come on, for Christ's sake," Quinn said, and he shot Muñoz high in the chest.

Susan Zago screamed. Quinn got himself turned quickly in the direction of the door, the pistol out in front of him. He couldn't see Muñoz, he couldn't take his eyes off the door. He couldn't release a breath and get another one, and he had the fear that Muñoz was going to shoot him. Susan Zago stood up in the dark. "You fuck. God damn you fuck," she screamed, and the door opened behind her. A body came into the frame very low, and there was a yellow and red flash and the room was full of noise, and Susan Zago was in silhouette, then knocked sideways as though someone had grabbed her shoulder and flung her out of the way. He put three rounds into the door opening and slid sideways, and whatever had been in the door went out and something metal hit on the floor, then everything stopped. Susan Zago was lying on her stomach in front of him, not moving or making a breathing sound. Muñoz began jabbering in Spanish, his face to the floor, the lantern leaking fluid so that a flame began to travel on the tiles. There was the hot metal smell in the air, and Quinn had a roaring in his ears, as though he was dying and could hear it coming. He pushed back to the wall and waited for the boy outside. He put the gun exactly where he had it before and let himself slide so that he was aiming the pistol up through his bent legs. Muñoz kept jabbering for a minute, then suddenly took a deep exhausted breath and exhaled in a way that made his lips flutter, and then he was quiet and the room was quiet.

He needed out, though he wasn't sure yet who was outside or how even to get to the door. There was a strong kerosene smell in the room now. Muñoz's pants had caught fire and begun to burn with a lazy yellow flame, and Quinn wanted outside before the flame lit the room. He pushed away from the wall and rolled toward the door. It was raining, and he couldn't hear a small sound distinctly. There was a machine gun on the floor, and when he looked through the door he saw someone was lying against the stone balustrade. The rain made a soughing noise and beat loudly on the skylight inside. He got on his stomach, squirmed onto the gallery facing the way he had come, and rolled behind the dead man. The dead man was the boy who had killed Bernhardt, his slick hair and the soft features slightly disarranged. The boy still smelled like disinfectant. He had been shot in the neck and the flesh of his arm was torn and he felt soft. His glasses were still on. Quinn peered up over the boy's chest toward the steps. There was no way to see both ends of the gallery, and there was no way to tell which direction anyone would take around the paseo. He waited what felt like ten minutes to see a movement. Water drained off the baluster and washed blood down the front of the dead boy's shirt, and Quinn realized if he lay any longer he would get caught in the building and somebody would shoot him.

He got on his feet and crept low along the balcony, gun out in front of him, and came round the steps. No one was there, though a gun was on top of the baluster. He knelt against the cold stone and listened for anything, the sound of footsteps or sirens or whistles or an engine in the street, and he could hear nothing to believe someone was coming or that the commotion had been noticed at all. He stood and looked down the second tier of the building through the rain and dark, and could see nothing. The door to the studio was invisible and nothing seemed out of order. Everything was just as it had been for ten minutes.

He walked down into the open court where the light was grainy, and through the archway to the street. He looked out the entry down Bustamante. He could see the glare of blue lights where the truck repairs were still working, but there were no figures in between. He stepped into the cool street, the gun in his shirt, and walked toward Susan Zago's car. It was a shuck, all of it, but you just couldn't tell from the outside. You had to go all the way inside to find that out, like Bernhardt had said, and then you were in too deep. He thought about Bernhardt saying how much everybody wanted to please his wife, and that the guerrillas never pleased and never *got* pleased. Muñoz, he imagined, had probably never been really pleased in his life, but still managed to look spoiled and disappointed when he got lit up, as if it was the first time in his life things had ever gone really bad, and he didn't like it. He'd probably been coping real well, Quinn thought, until that very moment.

At the corner of Jiquilipán a mound of garbage was piled outside a vegetable market. A movie was letting out up the street, the lights on the marquee yellow and flatted by the rain. The movie was playing *The Sound of Music*.

Everything seemed let out, all the tricks, and it was stupid to have a gun now. He looked down the empty street, then took the gun and pushed it in with the soft vegetable mulch as far as his arm would go, then started quickly up Jiquilipán without looking in any other direction but the one he was going. He wondered, as he walked, if he'd perfected something in himself by killing three people he didn't know, when he had come at the beginning, simply to save one, and if now he had pleased anybody anywhere. Though he thought if he hadn't pleased anybody, at least he'd tried to, and had performed it under control, and he hadn't coped so bad all by himself at the end. He thought, in fact, that he'd done fine.

28

Two men had begun dismantling a Willys in the street at 2:00 a.m. One stood while the other pried at the fenders with an iron bar, like a cow being skinned, then the duties were reversed. There was no reason for it Quinn could see, but they were making a big racket in the street. A blue bus sat in front of the government palacio, a black 8 painted on its roof. A pair of the white puttee soldiers stood in the zócalo watching the men peeling metal off the jeep, though after a time they wandered away into the shadows of the Portal and became invisible. The rain had quit and water had collected on the concrete promenades, and crows were asleep in the jacarandas. He sat at the window and watched the Centro for any activity he could feature as significant, but there wasn't any. He had taken too many pills now and he felt dead inside.

He had checked at the administración for a call from the consulate, but there had been none. He had gone back to the room, undressed, and gotten in the shower to wash the garbage off his arms, and for a long time he stood in the warm water and trembled until the water overcame the cold feeling and until he thought the worst of it was over. It was soldier shakes, and they always went away.

Rae had sat on the bed and watched while he buttoned his shirt in the white light. She had a pint of Cuervo Gold on the bed beside her. When he finished she said, "Where's your gun?" and looked at him distantly.

"It's gone," he said.

"Did you shoot somebody with it?" she said.

"Everybody," he said.

"What's about to happen?" she said.

He pulled the chair to the window and sat looking out at the zócalo bathed in the greenish rain light. "Nothing," he said. "We have to leave." He opened the tequila and took a drink. There wasn't much left.

"What about the police?" she said.

"They're not coming."

"Aren't we in trouble?"

"We're not in *anything*. We're just getting out of here tomorrow," he said. The rain had slacked, and he watched the streets around the zócalo for police vehicles.

"What about the consulate?" Rae said.

"They didn't call," he said. "We're out of time."

Rae's face was pale as though she had cried a long time and couldn't do it any more. "Did she kill Bernhardt?"

"They wanted the bucks," Quinn said. "They thought he'd get it first. That was all. So yeah." He had the same feeling of falling again, of being high up alone, trying to look down but not succeeding. He knew in a little while that would stop, like the scared shakes stopped.

"That's not *all*," Rae said calmly. "He ditched her, didn't he?" She paused. "Do you not want to talk to me about that?"

"Not very much," he said.

She lay on the bedspread and closed her eyes. "You're not to feel bad, though," she said. "I know how people get in trouble now."

"Bad luck," he said.

"No. It's bad character. It's very simple," Rae said. "But there's nothing you can do about it now."

"I'm sorry," he said. "I tried. But I'm really sorry."

✳

At four o'clock it was still dark. The air was misty before light. The marginales who had been dismantling the Willys had left with metal pieces tied together with strings. Rae was asleep on the bedspread. His clothes had begun to dry.

Rae turned on the bed and looked at him, the spread drawn around her shoulders in the chill. "What're we going to do in New Orleans?" she said.

"Go to the dogs," he said.

"You won't leave me to the guys in the plaid suits, will you?"

"Not a chance."

In the hall he heard footsteps on the tiles. She turned and stared at the globe in the ceiling.

"Do you just like me because I'm the best around?" she said. "I'm sorry to want to know that, I can't help it."

He listened to the footsteps approaching. "That sounds right," he said.

"Then that's fair," she said. "I just wouldn't like you ditching me for somebody you liked less."

"I couldn't like anybody less," he said, "and I couldn't like anybody any more. That's what I've learned since I was a kid."

She turned and faced him. "You thought you could live without me, didn't you?"

"I did a moment," he said.

"But you can't, can you?"

"No. I can't."

She lay on her back again and thought a moment. "Do you know what today is?" she said softly.

He was listening for the steps. He had no fear of them at all. "I must've lost track."

"It's your birthday," she said. "Isn't that odd? Do you think you're old enough to live your life now?"

Someone knocked at the door. The clerk stood in the hall nervously. Clerks didn't like the corridors after dark. "There is a call," he said softly. "Consulado americano. An emergencia in the prisión. You to come." He walked away down the empty hall.

200

"What did he say?" Rae said from the bed. "I didn't hear."

"It's a call. I'll have to see," he said.

"But you have to tell me something, though, right now," she said, staring at him oddly. Love seemed to him like a place to be, a place where nothing troublesome could come inside, not even Sonny's taking it down. "I just want to know how I look now," she said. She studied him seriously, afraid. "You see everything. I want to know." Her eyes were wet and her hair was bright around her face.

"Just great," he said.

"Wonderful?" she said. "Would you say wonderful?"

"Wonderful," he said.

"Do you think you're old enough to live your life unprotected, Harry?" she said. "You can't back off from what scares you."

"Nothing scares me," he said.

"Happy birthday, then," she said. "Happy birthday to you." She got out of bed to come with him.